THE CORNHUSK DOLL

WINNER OF DODD, MEAD
LIBRARIAN PRIZE COMPETITION

The
CORNHUSK DOLL

Eleanor Reindollar Wilcox

Illustrated by *Gerald McCann*

DODD, MEAD & COMPANY • NEW YORK • 1956

© 1956 by Eleanor Reindollar Wilcox
All rights reserved

No part of this book may be reproduced in any form without permission in writing from the publisher

Second Printing

Library of Congress Catalog Card Number: 56-5185

Printed in the United States of America
by The Cornwall Press, Inc., Cornwall, N. Y.

For George R. and David

ACKNOWLEDGMENTS

The author's grateful thanks for help and information used in writing *The Cornhusk Doll* go to:

The Enoch Pratt Free Library, Baltimore, Maryland, that never-failing fountain of information.

The Maryland Academy of Sciences, Baltimore, Maryland, whose Indian collection and library inspired this story in the beginning.

The Baltimore and Ohio Railroad Transportation Museum, Baltimore, Maryland, where a genuine Conestoga wagon can be studied.

The Maryland Historical Society, whose archives are a Godsend to the searcher.

All the cooperative people at the places mentioned, who are always willing and eager to serve the searcher.

And last but not least, the Park School of Baltimore—in order to enter this book in the Librarian's Award Contest, I had to be a Librarian! And I am very proud and happy to be the Park School's Upper School Librarian.

CONTENTS

1. THE WAGON — 1
2. MURRAY'S RANGE — 22
3. LADY GEORGEANNA GOES A-VOYAGING — 46
4. BEARS IN THE BERRY PATCH — 63
5. PRETTYING POLLY! — 78
6. THE CABIN IN THE FOREST — 97
7. "SHAWNEE!" — 118
8. WINTER WITH THE SHAWANO PEOPLE — 149
9. THE VOICE OF THE PANTHER — 161
10. AGAIN THE HOUSE IN THE FOREST — 169
11. HOME! — 179
12. THE GATHERING — 193
13. THE MESSAGE — 204

ILLUSTRATIONS

Benjamin Franklin called to her. "Not so fast, Miss Sally! Come back and let these gentlemen see the young lady who is going to ride a Conestoga wagon . . ." 11

The Bay was suddenly turned into a churning confusion of black water that tipped and tilted the plunging schooner like a toy boat. 31

Never could she forget that Nannie Tatum's onliest baby had been lost back there across the mountains. 61

And on the morning that Adam Byles found Indian sign, he let Sally hold the long rifle. 67

Sally dropped the pail and stared up into the leaves. Two little feet in deerskin moccasins were digging into the bark. 71

Sally thought she had never seen a toy so queer. Its body was made of cornhusks, tightly wrapped together. 75

She had been taken by some Shawnee three years ago, and her parents had simply disappeared.   *89*

Background map of the action of the story.   *100*

Only the thought of how the winter wind would howl through any unstopped cracks spurred her on.   *109*

She was dumb with terror and hardly knew that the silent warrior had picked her up like a bundle of blankets.   *117*

The Indian grunted in satisfaction. "All safe, now. Peace Woman has spoken," he said.   *125*

A white man! Sally's heart leaped. She wanted to run to him ... and beg him to take her to her parents.   *137*

"But you're my friends! You're my other family!"   *175*

The characters, incidents, situations and some of the places in this book are imaginary and have no relation to any person, place or actual happening. The historical places—Philadelphia, Baltimore, the western forts—are as accurate as contemporary accounts can make them. The incidents involving Mary Eliza McPhee are based on a number of similar cases in frontier history, but not on the experiences of any one person. The land troubles caused by the Proclamation Line affected the settlement of the Ohio Country very little. Like many other treaty articles, it was honored on paper.

THE CORNHUSK DOLL

CHAPTER 1

THE WAGON

THE BELLS on the horse harness were ringing a merry song. With every jolt and heave of the Conestoga wagon, they sounded out like the church bells of Philadelphia. *"Philadelphia! Philadelphia! We're leaving Philadelphia far behind!"* At least, that was what Sally Redpath thought they said. She was standing on the lazyboard beside the driver, with Lady Georgeanna Caroline Maltravers in her arms, watching the road ahead. It stretched like a ribbon of red and brown through the endless green of the forest. Sally was riding on the leading wagon because of Jacob Stoltzfus. He was the big Pennsylvania German with the beard, who stood beside her, staring straight ahead at the endless blue waves of the hills rolling away and away until they fetched up against the dark blue wall of the Alleghenies.

It was hard to understand Jacob, because of his queer half-German words, but Sally knew how much he liked her. He had three *"kleine Madchens"* of his own, back home in Lancaster. Of course, they were not to be mentioned in the same breath with his seven sons! Sally amused herself by naming them over when the sun shone hot and the road seemed endless.

"Karl, Jacob, Herman, Heinrich, Johann, Pieter, August. August, Pieter, Johann, Heinrich, Herman, Jacob, Karl!" And then, as if they didn't matter much, "Sannie, Sarie, Elizabetta!" Sally was glad she had a name like Sarah Caroline. She didn't know that thousands of little German girls, here in Pennsylvania and far across the sea in the Palatine Provinces and in all the little German duchies, too, were also named Sarah Caroline. Sally was Sarah Caroline Redpath, but if she had been Sarah Stoltzfus, she would have been Sarie-for-short.

Jacob and his neighbors around Lancaster were overly proud of their boys, Sally's father said. They seldom had a good word for all the blonde-headed little girls in their long dresses and aprons, hard at work in the kitchens with their big, silent mothers. Sally helped her mother, too, but she had never hoed corn and tobacco in the hot summer weather, like the girls on the farms. The Lancaster women worked very hard and raised babies, Sally's mother said, and got little enough thanks in this world. But Jacob Stoltzfus must have had a soft spot in his heart for *madchen,* since he let Sally ride up front with him. The Redpaths' big, white-topped wagon was back along the line. Sally and Lady Georgeanna rode in state where they could watch the road ahead.

And what an exciting journey it had been, so far! Sally wriggled her toes in her real Indian moccasins—another part of the adventure that seemed like a voyage into fairyland—and thought back over the past weeks. Surely no other little girl, ten years old in May of this wonderful year of our Lord 1764, had ever had such luck.

First of all, there had been that day during the past winter, when her father had come home to the big brick house on Broad Street, brimming over with news. He had come straight in to the fireside, where Sally was playing with the cat and her mother was embroidering on the frame. Hardly waiting for Caesar, the Negro man-servant, to take his cloak, he had cried, "It's all settled, Matilda! The grant has been cleared from his Lordship. We start for the Ohio lands as soon as the roads over the mountains are open."

Matilda Redpath had laid down her needle and her silken yarns. The lace on her London gown was creamy at her throat, where the brooch with the crest, inlaid with gold, held the folds of her neckerchief over the top of her stiff, brocaded bodice. She looked at Sally on the hearth rug in her dainty sprigged muslin gown.

"It's a far cry from Philadelphia, my dear," she said in her soft voice. "Are you set upon going?"

"Set upon it? Matilda, the Ohio Company will make men rich beyond their wildest dreams in the fur trade. Our Sally will live in a cabin for a time, but she'll marry a lord in London Town before ten years are out!"

And so it was that the very next day Sally had carried a note to prim Miss Collingwood at the Seminary for Genteel Young Females. It requested Miss Collingwood's permission to withdraw Miss Redpath at the close of the spring term. Withdraw Miss Redpath! No more tiresome embroidery lessons, no more French from twittery little

Monsieur, no more lectures on deportment from Miss Collingwood herself, terrible in a towering wig, and best of all, no more of that dreadful wire collar! The collar was the worst thing about the seminary. You put it on when you arrived at the door in the morning—Sally wondered if the boarding pupils donned theirs when they got up—and you wore it all day long, until Caesar's welcome knock at the door announced the end of another session for her. It was a horrid brace sort of thing, which kept your neck straight and stiff. You couldn't bend your head at all. You even wore it during dancing lesson. All the girls wore them, from tiny Phoebe Drexel, who was still at her hornbook, just spelling C-A-T, to beautiful Ann Dupre, fifteen years old and heiress to a tobacco planter's fortune in Virginia. Miss Collingwood's young ladies were famous for their swanlike necks and graceful manners. They also practiced walking with piles of books on their heads. That could be fun. Sometimes the piles wobbled and fell off with a crash. Once Miss Collingwood herself was hit by a flying Greek lexicon!

All the other girls were as wild with excitement over the trip to Ohio as Sally herself. To travel in a wagon over the western road, beyond safe York and Lancaster, into the Great Forest, where every tree hid a murderous Indian, all the way to Fort Cumberland and over the Great Blue Wall of the mountains to Fort Pitt! Why it was only yesterday that the Frenchies had held all that land and hired the Indians to scalp the English settlers and steal their children away to be Indians, too! Some of the girls pretended to be terrified at the very idea of such a dangerous journey, but Sally knew they were just jealous.

And Peggy McFarland, a redheaded girl from Raystown, daughter of a Scotch trader, cried a little when she heard the news. She wanted so badly to go home to her father's store in the stockaded fort. She felt all tame and fenced in here in calm Philadelphia, but her father was determined that she should have all the accomplishments of a young lady.

"I love the spring mornings when the squaws bring yarbs to trade for beads and red flannel," Peggy declared. "I'm jist—I mean just—as scairt—scared—of the Redsticks as anybody when they're a-skulkin' and a-scalpin', but they can be awful nice if they know a body. And oh, how I do miss the pipers of the Forty-second!"

The other girls laughed at Peggy, but Sally sought her company from then on. She asked a thousand questions about Indians and animals and birds and what kinds of trees and flowers she might find about the western woods. Miss Collingwood's young ladies pressed garden flowers in their albums—roses and verbena and lilies and ferns. Miss Collingwood felt there was something barbarous about American wildflowers. Jack-in-the-pulpit and bird's foot violet, dogwood and fringed gentian—they were all so beautiful, Sally thought. But Miss Collingwood never read elegant poetry about such blossoms. Young ladies should be able to recite gracious little sentiments about the flowers in their albums when they exhibited them to admiring visitors. Miss Collingwood had never heard any poem entitled *To the First Bloodroot in Spring*.

Neither did Miss Collingwood fully approve of bagpipes. They were a wild, outlandish instrument, played chiefly by those dreadful Highlanders, who only lately had come skirmishing into England, trying to put that scapegrace, Prince Charlie, on the throne. The fact that those same wild Highlanders were doing brave service out on the wild, desolate frontier, keeping the French and Indians off Miss Collingwood's doorstep, had not altered her opinion. They were only a couple of jumps above the savages, she felt, and their music was not to be compared with that of a well-tuned spinet.

Well, spring had come at last. Sally bade a damp farewell to her friends—the girls all cried like ninnies—and dropped a proper curtsey to Miss Collingwood.

"Farewell, Miss Redpath!" that grim lady had cried. "No matter into what wilderness you voyage, remember always that you are a Collingwood pupil!"

There was so much packing to be done! Matilda Redpath could hardly bear to see so many of her treasures bundled off to Uncle Jasper's big house. The highboys, the spinet, the great sideboard and the chairs that had come over with Grandsire Redpath from Surrey, fifty years or more ago—none of them could make the first trip over the mountains. Later, perhaps, when the new home was built, the furniture could be freighted out to them. Now they could take only the most necessary things. Caesar and old Callie, the cook, their tears dropping into the pots and pans, packed up the kitchen things. Copper kettles and iron trivets, saucepans and cauldrons and warming pans— all had to be stowed safely in the Conestoga wagon. Caesar and Callie would be turned over to kindly Uncle Jasper. They would follow the family over the Blue Ridge later on. Caesar wept because he felt sure his white folks would be lost without him. Callie's tears were for her poor Missie, cooking over campfires in a skillet!

In the end, all the things needed to start a home in the wilderness were assembled. The spinning wheel was there.

Her mother said to Sally, "I never thought I'd see the day when I'd touch a wheel again. Now you'll have to learn to card and spin, too. Maybe we raised you too fine."

There were two pieces of real furniture going along, if you didn't count the little footstool and the rush-bottomed chairs. One was the little old cradle. The other was the big, four-poster bed. Mother had insisted on that.

"I don't care if we leave the plow home, Henry," she had said firmly, "I am going to sleep on a decent feather bed at night. You may roll up in blankets among the bales and boxes, but Sally and I intend to be comfortable, even amongst the savages."

So the big four-poster had been taken downstairs, piece by piece, and stowed in the wagon. The feather tick was spread in the wagon bed. Every night, when they did not stop at a tavern, Mother had spread the quilts and blankets on it. Surely this was traveling in comfort!

The wagon itself was Sally's greatest joy, though. It was like an ark, loaded with pots and kettles, bedding and chairs, boxes and bales and even a carved chest that had come down in Matilda Redpath's family—she had been a Murray, of Baltimore. Henry Redpath had been in despair when his wife had insisted on wearing her beautiful Paris hat with the ostrich plumes.

"A hat like that among the Shawnees and Delawares! You'll see it adorning the chief medicine man before you're through."

But the Paris hat hadn't reached as far as the Shawnees and Delawares. Sally's mother had yielded it at Wright's Ferry, to an Irish washerwoman. There were the dirty clothes—piles of them! And there was Matilda Redpath, whose dainty hands had never pounded linen on stones in the Susquehanna River, or boiled water in an iron pot over a fire, or developed red cracks from the strong lye soap. Callie had always done such hard things as the washing for her. Sally giggled as she remembered how Bridget Concannon had stood, her capable hands on her broad hips, and stared at that wonderful hat. Green satin, it was, with green feathers that changed colors as the sun struck them.

"I'd wash the Angel Gabriel himself for the likes o' that hat, ma'am," she had declared.

Sally's mother had hesitated one instant . . . then, "It's a bargain," she said.

When the wagons had rolled westward from the Susquehanna the next morning, the Redpaths had a pile of freshly washed and ironed clothes—and Mother was wearing a straw hat, tied on with a red calico kerchief. Green feathers flying, Bridget Concannon was parading through Wright's Ferry on the arm of an awestruck sergeant of the American Rifles, while the other washerwomen of the regiment gazed at her, speechless with envy.

The wagon itself was the most wonderful thing! Of course, Sally had seen wagons like it all her short life, bringing cider and cheese and corn to the market in Philadelphia. They came from the lush farms where the German and Moravian settlers lived. The plump women with their full skirts and sunbonnets had cackling geese and squawking hens tucked under their arms. The stout, bearded men in their broad-brimmed hats stood on the lazy-boards behind the horses.

When Father had begun to plan the journey, he had decided at once on one of these wagons to carry his family over the mountains. Sally had been walking with him one day when they met Father's friend, Mr. Benjamin Franklin. Mr. Franklin was the printer who published the *Pennsylvania Gazette*. He was a most important person, Father said.

"Well, Henry, I hear you are all for the western country and the fur trade," Mr. Franklin had said.

"Yes, Ben," Father had answered, "and I'm off to Conestoga within the week to see about a wagon."

"Save yourself the trouble, Henry," Ben Franklin had replied. "You'll recall when General Braddock couldn't scrape together a dozen wagons to carry corn and oats to Will's Creek?"

"Aye, that I do. The army in the West was starving. It was you who published the ad in the *Gazette* that fetched the Dutch farmers in from the whole countryside with their wagons and horses."

"I acquired a pretty knowledge of wagons and wagoners that year," Ben Franklin went on, looking over his square spectacles to smile at Sally, who was hopping first on one foot and then on the other.

"I would advise you to hire yourself a wagon and team, rather than go to the expense of buying such a caravan, Henry. You will have no use for six horses in the Ohio country, unless you plan to become a teamster as well as a fur trader."

"Do you say so, Ben?" Henry Redpath was impressed. After all, the man who fills Poor Richard's Almanac with such wisdom as "A Penny Saved Is a Penny Earn'd" ought to know a saving when he sees one.

A few nights later, Sally was about to go up to bed when a discreet tapping came at the street door. Old Caesar hobbled to open it, letting a breath of chilly fog into the paneled hall. Sally, one foot on the bottom stairstep, saw three cloaked and hatted gentlemen standing on the doorstep, and who should be the foremost but Dr. Franklin, himself! Caesar bowed the callers in. Sally bobbed a curtsey and was going on up the stairs, but Benjamin Franklin called to her.

"Not so fast, Miss Sally! Come back and let these gentlemen see the young lady who is going to ride a Conestoga wagon to the Ohio country!"

Sally dutifully returned and was inspected by two tall men. One chucked her chin and called her a pretty wench. The other looked long and hard and said to Benjamin Franklin, "Redpath's not taking his family along, surely?"

"Aye, that he is," Dr. Franklin replied, handing Caesar his cloak and hat.

"Is he out of his mind? Mistress Redpath and this child in a mud-floored hovel in the forest?"

"He says that, if homes are established, civilization will quickly follow," Dr. Franklin answered.

" 'To make an omelette, one must break a certain number of eggs,' " the stranger quoted sourly.

"My dear Worthington," Benjamin Franklin chided,

Benjamin Franklin called to her. "Not so fast, Miss Sally! Come back and let these gentlemen see the young lady who is going to ride a Conestoga wagon..."

"are you inferring that the Redpaths are to be compared with Peter's peasants?"

But then Father came out of the library, and swept the visitors in, with a torrent of bows and "your servant, sirs."

"Miss Sally, you best run along to bed," Caesar warned her.

Callie appeared at the head of the stairs, candle in hand. "Come along, child," she ordered. "I got your bed all warmed. Don't waste them coals on me."

Sally ran upstairs. Callie helped her out of her clothes before the fireplace in the big front bedroom. The trundle-bed, which was pushed under the big four-poster by day, was now pulled out onto the floor alongside. Sally's night-rail, a linen gown which hung to her toes, was warming in front of the fire. Callie filled a china basin with water from a small copper kettle, kept warm on an iron holder in the angle of the fireplace. Sally, nightgowned and swathed in a knitted shawl, perched on a hassock while Callie washed her face, hands and feet. All-over baths were for special occasions and hot weather. Callie brushed her fair, straight hair until Sally's eyes filled with tears and her head ached from the strain of pulling against the brush.

"I brushes and brushes," Callie complained, "but no curls come. Got to keep hair like this jus' like silk to give it any looks at all. Come time to put some curls in, we gonna have our troubles."

She thrust the copper warming-pan, a long-handled contraption filled with hot coals, between the sheets for the second time. She slid it rapidly back and forth, felt the linen, and pulled it out.

"In you goes," she commanded, and Sally, dropping the shawl, dived into the trundle-bed.

Mother appeared, her cashmere shawl about her.

"Lud, how the damp does go through my bones tonight," she complained, backing up to the fire and spreading her skirts to catch the heat.

"Ain't a patch on how it goin' through your bones in the big woods," Callie snorted. "Craziest nonsense I ever heard. Mast' Henry can go get hisself sculped and friz and roasted—let him go! Plenty men does. Why cain't we stay here in peace and comfort whiles he prowlin' mongst Injuns and wolves?"

Sally sat up in bed.

"Mother," she asked, hugging her wooly comforter to her, "who was Peter who broke eggs to make an omelette?"

Matilda Redpath and Callie stared at the child in complete bewilderment.

"This Peter pusson ain't the only one break aggs to make omelette," Callie said. "You-all know any other way?"

"What do you mean, child?" Mother asked.

"One of the gentlemen who came to see Father said it," Sally answered. "I think he was talking about us. He seemed to be angry at Father because we were going along."

Matilda Redpath frowned.

"I don't know what he meant, lovey," she said, as she knelt beside the bed. "We'll ask your father in the morning. Now say your prayers and go to sleep."

But long after Mother and Callie had left the room, Sally lay watching the firelight flicker on the ceiling. Far down the street, the voice of the town watchman pierced the darkness.

"Ten o' the clock, an' a thick, foggy night! Ten o' the clock—"

Sally drifted off to sleep seeing herself and Mother swimming desperately in a sea of half-beaten eggs. Befeathered Indians were breaking more and more eggs and pouring them in. Mr. Worthington stood disapprovingly by and muttered over and over, "To make an omelette, one must break a certain number of eggs—"

Sally asked a good many people about Peter and the eggs before she finally got her answer. It was at school, of all places. Master Otterbein, who tried to teach the young ladies rhetoric and philosophy, was rambling on as usual. Sally, half-dozing, was thinking of her French lesson—a nursery rhyme about a bridge in some far place called Avignon, where people danced forever on the bridge itself. In French class, she would think of Master Otterbein's ears—like teacup handles, they were. . . . Suddenly, the teacher said something that brought her wide-awake.

"And do you know, young ladies, what this iron-souled despot said? Thousands, aye, tens of thousands of Russians died in the swamps of the Neva ere St. Petersburg was builded. His ministers pled with him. 'What is a city, compared to the lives of your people?' they asked. And what replied the Czar of All the Russias? 'To make an omelette, one must break eggs!' "

Sally's mouth flew open. An expression of mingled horror and delight came over her face.

"Horrible, is it not? Yes, Miss Redpath, I do not wonder that such sentiments rouse dismay in your tender mind. And yet, when it was over, there stood a city created out of the blood and tears of a nation!"

Sally thought she understood what Mr. Worthington meant. He felt that her Mother and she would be smashed to help Father build a fortune on the frontier! Did any of Peter's poor egg-people mind very much? Sally wondered. It was too big a problem to worry about. She decided that, come what may, she would not let herself be smashed!

Other gentlemen came and went, interested in Father's venture in varying degrees. When Father explained that he was willing to leave his flourishing business in the capable hands of Uncle Jasper Redpath, and take a risk in the fur trade, most of his acquaintances thought him rash indeed. The Ohio Company had been founded before the wars, when men of all nations were pushing into the new lands beyond the Blue Ridge Mountains. The Company had probably helped to start the trouble, although that was bound to come anyway, with France and England each trying to grab the rich fur trade. Mr. Worthington in particular felt that the thing to do was to send out capable trappers and traders to do the actual work, while Father acted as manager or factor.

"Agreed, agreed, dear Worthington," said Father, over a bowl of hot mulled wine one evening just before their departure. "But if I do not go over the actual ground, see the land myself, establish my right to the grant, how can I be sure that I will not be cheated, nay, robbed outright by some frontier cutthroats or connivers?"

"Indeed, Redpath, I agree that that is a sound idea, but why, in Heaven's name, man, leave your fine home in

Philadelphia and settle in the wilderness? An inspection tour once a year, surely that will be enough? You don't see the Harmons or the da Silvas riding into the forest, and they make thousands every year out of beaver. I doubt if old Mendez da Silva knows a Mingo from a Delaware, or a slippery elm from a grapevine, but he hires the men who do!"

"Well, if you must know, sir," Father said slowly, "it is because from my boyhood up I have had a passion to see what lay beyond the mountains. If I own those acres in the western lands today, it is because, when I was a lad, my father sent me to London to finish my education. Every Englishman seems to think that we grow feathers on our heads and dine with the Mohawks. And here I was, a lad from pleasant Philadelphia, who knew no Indians but our tame Lenapes, and what answers could I give to all their questions?"

"Aye, they think us barbarians," said Mr. Worthington. "They forget 'tis well nigh two centuries since Englishmen first planted these shores."

"And shores they will remain, unless more of us strike out for the interior of this vast continent!" said Dr. Franklin, who entered at that moment, with Sally at his heels.

She curtsied to the company, who bowed to her as gravely as if she had been a young lady.

"I was not listening at the door, Father," she whispered, as she came around the inlaid mahogany table to his chair. "I did but come to bid you good night."

"And met me coming in." Dr. Franklin smiled. "Spring is in the air tonight, my friends. I trust it is the springtime of our hopes, as well."

"That's my little Sally," Father said. "She never forgets her duty to her father, gentlemen. Good night, poppet. Pray tell your mother I'll be sitting up late with these gentlemen."

"Father—I couldn't help hearing you say—you started to tell about how you came to own the land we're going to. Could you finish telling so I could hear, also?" Sally perched on the arm of his chair with a pleading look on her face.

"Aye, tell us, Henry," said Benjamin Franklin, taking the chair by the punch bowl. "Let the lass stay. I'll warrant our discourse will be the soberer for her presence!"

"Well, Sally, it happens that our cousin, Peveril Redpath, is secretary to one of the Penn family—and was twenty years ago, when I was fresh out of the university. He was most kind to his young American cousin and made me known to many gentlemen at court. It was in that casual way that I came to know the Earl of—shall we say Bangor, gentlemen, since that is not his title? His Lordship wishes to be nameless in this transaction."

"This has quite the air of a mystery, Henry," the second gentleman declared, smiling knowingly.

"May I venture a guess?" asked Dr. Franklin. "Since I go to St. James in the autumn, to advance the cause of the colonies, it would be but amusing to look up the gentleman and tell him his generosity is bearing fruit twenty years since—"

"Nay, nay," Father answered. "I will not reveal his name. He is a man who ever stands opposed to the House of Hanover, and 'twill do no good to any of us to bandy his name about. That means, my Sally, that the Earl had no liking for German King Georgie, and twenty years ago that might have meant his head."

"Oho, a Jacobite," said Mr. Worthington.

"Well, be that as it may, one dark night, as I was returning to Cousin Redpath's, I heard shouts for help and a great hurroosh of cries, and thinking someone was set upon by footpads—the streets of London were infested by night by the scurviest crew of skulkers and cutpurses a city ever held—"

"And still are," said Benjamin Franklin.

"I ran up, hallooing for the watch as I came, and saw two men engaged in beating a third, who was holding his own well enough, but in need of succor. I lunged at the first bravo with my sword, and he, having little stomach for the steel, took to his heels. But to my surprise, the intended victim, who by now had got his second wind, laid the other nightwalker flat on the tiles and said to me, 'Not the watch, sir. Let us leave the villain to them, forsooth, and be out of here speedily.'

"He drew me after him, down the dark areaway and into the next street, where we found lights and crowds of passers-by, and then I saw that my gentleman was the Earl. I was as astonished as he, but he made me understand that the attack was a matter of politics, and he had been set upon by men in the employ of a highly placed personage who would stop at nothing to put him out of the way. He had foolishly ventured abroad in an unfrequented street alone—and nearly paid dear for his folly.

"Well, to make a long story short, he invited me to a private meeting of some friends who were in the same way of thinking as he. It turned out that the attack on him had been planned to do more than frighten the Earl —this time, it was his death that was connived at, and I had saved his life. A turn of events made it impossible for his noble enemy to try again. But I had no wish to be drawn into any plottings—and the air was rife with them, what with the Young Pretender hovering in France, ready to rouse the Scots for himself. I begged to be excused from any conspiracies. Of course, as a gentleman, I gave my word that I would tell no one that I had seen the three fighters together. The next day, a messenger brought me the papers and the deed of gift to five hundred acres in the colony of Pennsylvania."

"My dear Redpath, that was no reward—that was a bribe!" Mr. Worthington laughed. "Does Governor Penn know that five hundred of his acres were handed out by a Jacobite plotter? Oh, be careful of your neck, Henry!"

"And just where are these acres located?" asked the other gentleman. "If they lie beyond the Proclamation Line, they may do you no good whatever—"

"The land was deeded before the treaty was made."

During the argument that followed, Sally slipped away upstairs, sure of but one thing, that Father's land might belong to him on paper, but it was quite another matter to find it and build a house on it.

The result of all this was that Benjamin Franklin had sent around Jacob Stoltzfus to see Father. Jacob had come, driving the wagon and the six horses, the bells chiming merrily and the harness all gleaming. Sally had never been inside one of these wagons before. She was enchanted with the big Conestoga. No wonder people called them *ships of the wilderness!*

The spotless white canvas cover, the brilliant red sideboards, the bright blue wagon-body with its vermilion underparts, its huge wheels with the great iron hubs, the wrought-iron jack, for hoisting it up to fix those same great wheels, the blue feedbox across the rear—all brand new!

"It's lovely! I never saw so fine a wagon in all my days!" Sally exclaimed.

The little girl got underfoot so much while Father and Jacob were coming to terms that they finally lifted her up and set her down inside. The interior of the wagon was roomy enough for a house, Sally thought. Indeed, Jacob Stoltzfus was saying that ten tons of freight could be carried in this selfsame wagon. It would take five weeks and three days, from Philadelphia to Fort Pitt, with no danger —"vell, practikal no danger, Herr Redpath, from the Indians, now that the troubles are over." There would be plenty of room for the rush-bottomed chairs, the Queen Anne bed, the tools, the clothing, everything needed to start a home in the wilderness. The tall clock would most certainly stand up inside. The ironbound trunks of Spanish leather would be lashed along the sides for ballast, lashed so that they would not shift and slide as the wagon lurched over the ruts and pitfalls of the western road.

The ringing chimes of the horse bells in particular delighted Sally. Jacob's horses—six big Conestogas, of the deep-chested, short-necked breed peculiar to the Conestoga valley—carried four brass bells apiece, strung across a light, arched frame above their heavy leather collars. Had Jacob wanted to, he could have hung frames of bells all over his team—he had pulled so many teamsters out of the mud on the road. The custom was that the rescued wagoner must give one of his sets of bells to the driver who pulled him out. Jacob, no doubt, had a barnful of bells home in Lancaster.

Had Sally been a boy, Jacob couldn't have been kinder, once he saw how she loved his wagon. He was as proud—maybe more so—of it as he was of his huge family. And that was how Sally came to stand on the lazy-board beside him, at the head of the procession crawling across the Alleghenies, pushing just one more spearhead of moving people into the silent green world of the endless forest.

While Jacob's fine wagon was bearing the Redpath outfit into the Ohio Country, back down the line, Jacob himself, because of his lofty position among the wagoners, was given the honor of driving the lead wagon. That it happened to be one of his second-best wagons, may have been merely a coincidence. It was toting barrels of flour to the garrison at Fort Pitt. Jacob was making a nice profit out of this trip.

CHAPTER 2

MURRAY'S RANGE

For a while it looked as if the Redpath section of the westward caravan would never get as far as Baltimore, let alone the western lands. Had Jacob Stoltzfus not been earning more from this trip than from his ordinary journeys, he would have protested violently at the backtracking made necessary by Mother and her determination to pay a last visit to Murray's Range. Sally thought everything was settled when they rolled out of Wright's Ferry. The crossing of the Susquehanna River was behind them. The wash was done for weeks ahead, from the looks of the pile that Mother had sorted and put away in the chests. The wagons creaked along steadily, the horses urged and impelled by torrents of German. Father rode alongside of Jacob's own wagon, at the head of the line, gazing happily westward at the dim blue hills. Suddenly Sally, running full speed from the Redpath wagon to catch up with the leaders, called breathlessly to him,

"Father! Mother would speak to you at once!"

Henry Redpath reined in and looked down at his breathless little daughter.

"What's amiss?"

"I don't know, but she is fretted about something."

Father turned back, while Sally waited beside the trail. There was a long discussion between her parents, and by the time that Sally got back into their wagon again, Father was red and indignant, but Mother was crying.

"What's wrong?" Sally asked, as she was lifted aboard.

"Matilda, I cannot ask this of Stoltzfus," Father was saying. "I've contracted with the man to carry us to the Ohio. He will not want to turn aside now."

"Henry," Mother said, "I have agreed to come with you on this mad journey. The farther from home we get, the surer am I that we'll ne'er see Philadelphia again. Is it asking so much that we drop down to Baltimore Town to see my mother that I may never see again in this world?"

"Then why in Heaven's name must you wait until we have crossed the Susquehanna to be overcome with a feeling that you'll ne'er see home again? This was all thrashed out a month since."

Mother clenched her fingers tightly in her lap.

"If Jacob Stoltzfus wants to back out, there are other wagoners who will like the color of my gold," Mother said.

Sally was alarmed. She had never heard Mother talk this way before. Father chewed his lower lip in silence. Then he slapped his horse on the flank with his hat and trotted off toward the head of the train to find Jacob.

Strange to say, Jacob Stoltzfus only shrugged his broad shoulders. Mother was right. A longer journey meant more pay to the thrifty wagoner, certainly more than he would normally earn. In a short time, everything was settled. Hans Oberholtzer, Jacob's companion, took over the leadership of the small caravan. Jacob turned his cargo of flour barrels over to him, climbed the lazy-board of the Redpath Conestoga, and turned the heads of the team eastward again, toward the river.

They caused some comment returning through Wright's Ferry, but Mother sat bolt upright, very proud and distant, Father rode beside the wagon in glum silence, the cow plodded sulkily at the wagon tail, and Sally peered at passers-by in vain hopes of spotting Bridget in the hat.

The roads being what they were, it was necessary to follow the east bank of the river clear down to the head of Chesapeake Bay, where boats could be gotten for Baltimore. Frenchtown was a busy little community that made its living ferrying passengers and freight.

"If only you had determined upon this visit before we left home," said Father for the tenth time, surveying the waterfront in despair, "we could have come straight down a good road and have been in Baltimore days gone by."

"Yes, Henry," said Mother quietly. "It was just a feeling that grew on me. Call it what you will, but I can go to the wilderness in peace, once I have been home."

Jacob Stoltzfus and Henry Redpath exchanged glances as if to say, so it looked to Sally, "Women!" She squirmed uncomfortably. Glad as she was of a chance to visit Grandmother Murray, she wished her family had settled all this before they left home.

Father and Jacob had little trouble getting a boat for Baltimore. Early in the morning, wagon, horses, the Redpaths, Jacob Stoltzfus and some twenty-odd passengers were loaded aboard the schooner *Day's Eye,* with as much confusion and scramble as would have loaded a small army.

It was a fine, clear morning, and the tree-lined banks of the river receded rapidly as the schooner's sails caught the breeze. Sally, entranced at the whole procedure, stood as close to the prow as she could get. She was underfoot when the crew, consisting of a lanky lad of sixteen and two Negro men, in canvas trousers slashed off below the knees, let go the jib sheets. She stood beside the mate, a sunburned waterman in a wide straw hat, as he shouted to the boys to look lively. She dashed aft to gaze in awe at the captain, a grizzled man with real gold earrings, who had spent his life between Turkey Point and Cape Henry, but dreamed of the Spanish Main as much as any boy who dreams of pirate treasure. He was at the wheel, squinting at the horizon from under his flat-brimmed tarred hat. Sally, whose voyaging had been confined to the Delaware River—she had been less than two years old when last she visited Grandmother Murray—was in raptures over the wide expanse of water that danced in the sun.

"Is this truly the Chesapeake Bay, sir?" she asked, spreading her feet in imitation of the captain, although the schooner rode the waves with a smooth, forward glide that required no sea legs whatever.

"Aye, Miss, that it is," he answered.

"I meant—that is—does it stop being the Susquehanna River just hereabouts?"

"Well, there's them as says it does, and them as says it don't," he responded, waving loftily to a passing ketch, which saluted by blowing a fish horn. "Some says as how the river goes clear down off the mouth of the Patapsco afore the Bay starts, but that's lallygaggle if ever I heard it."

"It stands to reason, Cap'n, that this ain't the Bay," argued the mate, who had ambled aft in his bare feet. "Why, this ain't salt water up here. Nary an oyster bar. All these rivers 're dumpin' fresh water in." He proceeded to tick them off on his fingers for Sally's benefit. "Susquehanna, Elk, North East, Sassafras, Bohemia—why it's all rivers and no Bay. Sho' the Bay begins down off the Patapsco. Even the feesh knows that."

Sally giggled. An osprey swooped low over the schooner, beating upwind toward his nest on a tall dead pine ashore.

"Watch that there ol' feesh hawk," said the mate. "Bet he don't make it home."

"Why not?" asked Sally, craning to watch the big bird.

"See that teenchy speck way up yonder?"

Sally squinted obediently into the dazzling dome above and, after a moment, located a dark something no bigger than a dust grain.

"Keep your eye on him," said the mate.

Sure enough, the dark speck descended with blinding speed, became a small bird, a huge bird, a plummeting bolt of feathered lightning.

"Oh, it's an eagle!" cried Sally, in amazed delight.

"Feesh for breakfast," remarked the captain.

Down like a thunderstroke came the eagle, and the osprey, clutching his fish desperately, dodged and wove in a frantic effort to escape. The bald robber's claws were almost there—the osprey swooped out from under, the fish shot downward, the eagle sheered off in triumph, dove onto the falling prize—and leveled off with the stolen catch in his talons.

"Oh, the poor fish hawk!" Sally cried. "That's a shame, I do declare."

"He's used to it. Happens every day," the mate said. "Now he'll go fetch home another whilst Master Baldy is a-feasting."

"Like a privateer pouncing on a fat merchantman," the captain remarked.

"Oh, were you ever on a privateer?" Sally gasped.

"Sho' he was," said the mate, genially. "Signed on as cabin boy when he was a younker o' twelve. Ended up with a chest o' gold."

"What did he—you—do with it all?"

"Had it melted down to make these here earrings," the captain said, his eyes fixed on the mainsail, which had begun to flap. He edged the wheel over and headed the schooner into the wind a little.

"She won't hold, Jeremy," he said to the mate. "Wind's droppin'."

"Nice day to be becalmed," Jeremy said.

They could see the glassy surface of the water smooth out ahead where the last ripples died. The schooner rocked gently, her sails hung almost limp. Sally spent the next several hours pestering Father, who paced the deck as impatiently as if he were the post rider bearing important dispatches that could change the fate of nations.

Mother had retired to the cabin, where she sat with a number of passengers among the piled-up boxes, trunks and baggage of the travelers for Baltimore. Jacob Stoltzfus had sat himself down on deck in the shelter of the Conestoga wagon. His six horses, protesting with rolling eyes and flattened ears their imprisonment on this strange wooden shed that rose and fell gently beneath their nervous hoofs, were secured in a horse pen near the bow of the schooner. But poor Jacob looked wan and green.

"What ails him?" asked Father, pausing in his promenade from bow to stern.

"He looks vastly queer," said Sally.

"It iss the poat," Jacob groaned. "Alvays I am up-coming ven the poat rocks."

"But she's not rocking, Jacob. It's a dead, flat calm—we're scarce moving!"

"Poats iss poats," he said glumly, and laid down on the deck.

The company refreshed themselves with cold meat, bread and other victuals brought out of roomy baskets. It was as much fun as a picnic, Sally thought, munching gingerbread that had hardly begun to get stale.

"When will we get to Baltimore?" she asked Jeremy, who was leaning on the starboard rail, chewing the stem of a long, clay pipe.

"Six hours or six weeks," he growled, "depends on the wind."

"It's got to blow a good wind, I want to get there! I'm in a hurry to see my grandmother. I haven't seen her since she came to our house in Philadelphia when I was but six years old. She lives on Murray's Range. Do you know where that is, Master Jeremy?"

"Can't say as I do," he replied. "But if you're in such a hurry to get there, you could whistle for some wind."

"Oh, but I mustn't whistle," Sally said. "Miss Collingwood says no young lady ever whistles. It's not genteel."

"Then I reckon we're just stuck here. We-uns whistled, and nothing happened. Did it, Pearl?"

"Nawsuh, Mast' Jeremy," one of the Negro hands answered with a grin.

"If you was to whistle, now, Missy," the mate continued, "might make just that much difference—might come up a wind. Mind you, now," seeing the mighty pucker Sally was attempting, "we don't want no gale, just a fair wind!"

Sally puckered up and blew. It was a pretty fair whistle that came out, considering Miss Collingwood's ban on whistling. Captain and crew stared solemnly out over the water. The sixteen-year-old lad took the wheel. Grayling, the big Conestoga horse, neighed indignantly in the horse pen. Jacob Stoltzfus groaned.

"Keep trying," said the captain. "I see a smidgen of wind over yonder by the point, or my name ain't John Pigeon."

Thus encouraged, Sally whistled again.

"Try a tune. Do *Soldier's Joy*," suggested Father, sarcastically.

Sally took a long breath, and did just that. Mother, emerging from the cabin, frowned at the group by the rail. She shook her head reprovingly at her daughter.

"It's for a wind, Mother," Sally explained.

"Even a lady may whistle for a wind," said Father, shading his eyes with his hand. "Is that a cat's-paw I see?"

"A which?"

"Cat's-paw—wind ripples on the water."

"Well, I hope so," said Mother. "Sally, you must not

make a nuisance of yourself. Come and sit down for a while."

Sally's wind was a time in coming, but when it came, it was more than they had bargained for! Shortly after noon, a line of black clouds came marching up over the horizon, level as a ruler, except where one vast billow of thunderhead reared itself.

"Squall coming!" the captain muttered. "Make fast them hosses." He took over the wheel while the crew helped Jacob secure the horses against the blow that was coming.

The bright surface of the Bay turned oyster-color and then leaden gray. The first puffs of the wind, blowing fitfully from every quarter, first flapped, then filled the sails. The schooner shook herself like a racer awakening from slumber. As the mainsail swelled, she heeled over, the white water hissed under her keel, ladies in the cabin squealed and grabbed for their sliding bundles, and Jacob Stoltzfus's miseries caught up with him.

The storm bore down on them with a rushing swish of rain. The placid Bay was suddenly turned into a churning confusion of black water that tipped and tilted the plunging schooner like a toy boat.

Father caught Sally under one arm as he slid headlong into the tilting cabin, bringing a fine gush of angry foam cascading in with him. Matilda Redpath, huddled in a corner with a plump country woman and a crate of chickens, both squawking, turned worried eyes on him.

"Is it bad?" she asked anxiously. "It feels dreadful! Are we in any danger?"

"No, no," Father assured her, putting Sally down on a

The Bay was suddenly turned into a churning confusion of black water that tipped and tilted the plunging schooner like a toy boat.

dry spot, "It's only a squall—the captain says it will be over in an hour."

"I truly didn't mean to whistle up such a storm!" Sally cried, shaking her drenched skirts like a dog shaking off bathwater. "Oh, Father, poor Jacob Stoltzfus! He has crawled up into the wagon. I think he's lying on our feather bed."

"Oh, dear me!" Mother cried. "I hope he will be careful—"

There was a great pounding of feet on the deck, as the crew raced to take in sail, Captain Pigeon's voice could be heard yelling commands. The rolling and pitching increased, thunder cracked and rumbled overhead. Just when the passengers were sure that they would be plunged into a watery grave, the cabin was flooded with sunlight, the hatch cover was thrown open to admit a draught of rain-washed air, and Jeremy bellowed cheerfully,

"How fare ye? Squall's over and a fair wind for Baltimore!"

"The Chesapeake Bay can kick up more tarnation fuss in short order than a woman with fits," the captain remarked calmly, as Sally emerged to watch the bank of storm clouds receding across the water toward the Eastern Shore.

"And here comes the Rock Hall ferry with her jib blown all to flinders," said Jeremy. A small ketch was crossing their bow, some half a mile ahead, the tatters of her jib flapping sadly. She continued on her course southwesterly, her two passengers waving their hats, her steersman saluting with a wave of the hand.

"Somebody bound for Annapolis got wet," said the captain.

"Be dry when they get there."

Jacob Stoltzfus climbed weakly down from the wagon and leaned over the rail.

"Mein vader coom over from the Palatinate. He told me to shtay away from ships. He vass right."

Late in the afternoon, driven swiftly on by a spanking breeze, the *Day's Eye* entered the Patapsco. The surface of the water was dotted with the sails of all sorts of craft— Jeremy pointed them out to Sally. Pungies, snows, sailing canoes, ketches, sloops, schooners—and, wonder to behold, a handsome full-rigged merchantman, flying her homeward-bound pennant, swept past them out to the open Bay, bound for Liverpool and old England.

The green shores drew together. Farms and buildings dotted the low banks. Sally could see the spars of ships against a background of low hills. The red roofs of houses appeared, plumes of smoke from numerous chimneys, church steeples pricked the air.

"This is Baltimore?" Sally asked.

"It's rightly three towns in one," Jeremy told her. "That there's Jones Town, where that stream comes down to the basin, and that there just beyond is Fell's Point, and across the basin is Baltimore Town."

"Baltimore Town!" Matilda Redpath, flushed and eager, stood at the port rail. She had tilted the country straw at the same pert angle at which she would have worn the green satin with the feathers. She wore a lace scarf which she had dug out of the Spanish trunk. Arriving in this bustling port was a little different from pulling in at a country tavern. This was home to her. Her childhood had been spent just beyond those first low hills, on Grandsire Murray's broad acres along Jones' Falls.

"But how it has grown!" Matilda Redpath exclaimed. "Look at all those new houses west of the wharves! Why, there're streets laid out where cornfields were! Why, it's nearly as large as Annapolis, Henry!"

"Bless me, it will soon be as large as Philadelphia," said Henry Redpath. He went over to where Jacob Stoltzfus was sitting up with his back against a big wagon wheel. Jacob groaned, then hauled himself to his wobbly feet.

"Vell, it iss ofer," he sighed. "Better ten thousand Redsticks dan der Chezapeag Bay!"

The *Day's Eye* dropped anchor alongside the public wharf. It was an imposing looking pier, to be sure, since it was almost a thousand feet long.

"Quite a long haul for foot passengers," Jeremy said, as the gangplank was lowered by the two Negro lads. "Had to build her that long to get over the ma'sh. Only thing wrong with Baltimore Harbor—shallow and muddy. The Point's got the deep anchorages."

By the time Jacob had the team harnessed and the Conestoga off the boat, the rest of the passengers had plodded ashore. Sally bid the captain and crew good-by and thanked them for such an interesting boat ride.

"Pleasant journey to ye all," John Pigeon shouted, as the Redpath party rumbled off up the long wharf to the streets of Baltimore Town.

Jacob Stoltzfus and the Conestoga were to put up at the Indian Queen Tavern. Father hired a boy to ride posthaste out of town to Murray's Range with the news of their arrival.

"Your mother will be taken quite aback, I fear," he said to his wife. "She thinks us well along on the western road by now."

Sally was sitting in the parlor of the Indian Queen while Mother sipped a cup of tea. Having gained her way about the Baltimore visit, she was completely happy, and merely smiled at her husband.

"She'll be so glad to see us she won't care if we dropped from the skies."

"Mother, will there be a pony for me to ride?" wondered Sally. "Tell me about the one you had when you were a little girl—"

The moon had risen high in the sky when the messenger boy returned. He came into the inn parlor, followed by a tall, elderly Negro man whose face lighted up at sight of Matilda Redpath.

"Miss 'Tilda! It's good to see you!"

"Abram! You haven't changed a bit! Oh, Abram, this is Miss Sally. Sally, this is our Abram. He carried you in his arms when you were a wee baby."

Sally shyly put out her hand to the old Negro, who bowed over it with the dignity of a duke.

"You is a young lady now, Miss Sally," he said. Then, having made his manners to Mast' Henry, he asked the family to follow him outside.

A light chaise pulled by a brown mare was waiting in the tavern yard. A small Negro boy mounted on a colt bobbed politely at them from where he sat on a square of old blanket, a lighted lantern in his free hand.

The chaise was big enough to hold Mother and Sally in comfort, being almost like a big covered chair on wheels, but Father had to ride behind with the small chest of valuables and clean clothes. Mother took the reins with a little cry of "This is like old times!" Old Abram mounted the colt, after the boy had slid back to sit on its rump as easily as if he had grown there. Sally laughed out loud at the sight they made, jogging out Long Street with the lantern bobbing before them like an overgrown firefly in the darkness.

"That must be Dilsy's boy," Mother decided. "What was his name? Hiram? Cyrus? James—yes, this is James. He was a yard-baby the last time I saw him!"

"What's a yard-baby?" Sally wanted to know. It was cozy, bouncing along in the mild darkness with Mother's lace shawl tickling her cheek, the mare's tail rising like a stiff plume ahead of them, and the lighted windows of the town sliding by in the spring night.

The feeling of adventure that came with riding in the Conestoga was replaced for the time by the pleasant, dreamy sensation of riding home to Grandmother's house.

"Dilsy used to say she had her children in sets of three— a lap-baby to nurse, a porch-baby to crawl, and a yard-baby to toddle about outside," Mother said, while Sally's head bobbed—bobbed—and finally fell hard against Mother's shoulder.

She was conscious of nothing more until the jogging stopped in a burst of light and welcoming voices, and Father lifted her down to be caught in the arms of a little lady in a frilled white cap, who cried, "Welcome, welcome to Murray's Range! Oh, child, how you have grown!" A rich smell of roasting chicken and new-baked bread filled the air. All grandmothers' houses smell of food and comfort, Sally thought, making her best curtsey with eyes still full of sleep.

Even in the darkness, Sally could see that the broad, comfortable farmhouse was very different from their formal brick mansion in Philadelphia. Two huge chimneys seemed to carry the house between them. Candlelight twinkled at deep-recessed windows. A wide porch ran across the front of the building. The winding drive was bordered with huge, dark boxwood bushes that filled the air with their rich scent.

Sally was hustled upstairs with Mother, Grandmother and a tall Negro woman who turned out to be Dilsy. She was washed amid a babel of loving laughter, questions, exclamations and suchlike. Mother perched like a little girl on the patchwork coverlet of a big feather bed, while Grandmother sat in a carved armchair with a faded velvet cushion worked in some heavy embroidery stitch. Presently a tap at the door announced a beaming young Negro girl— Dilsy's Agnes—with a tray piled high with a supper, all for Sally!

"I reckoned, being tired, you'd want to eat upstairs and go to sleep," Grandmother Murray said, as Dilsy fixed a little table with fine old linen, well-darned, but spotless, and thin silver spoons with the Murray crest on them. Sally enjoyed picking the drumstick and nibbling the flaky biscuits, swimming with homemade butter and strawberry jam.

When the grown-ups had gone away downstairs again, and Sally was put to bed in the feather tick—on such a warm night, she needed only the sheet over her—she lay listening to the whippoorwills in the woods behind the house. She was sunk in a deep peace made even deeper by the spell of the old house and the bed that had been Matilda Redpath's when she was a young girl on Murray's Range.

The roosters waked Sally to a sunny morning, and almost before she had stretched and was sitting up, little Agnes was peeking in the half-open door.

"Mornin' Missy," she said. "I fotched your hot water up."

She carried in a china pitcher and basin, and Sally lost no time in getting washed and dressed. She had a whole day on a farm to look forward to and she hurried through breakfast—a notable meal, with fried ham, beefsteak and fresh fish—so as not to miss anything. A tall, sunburned man who was introduced as Mr. Dorsey, a neighbor, was at the table with the family. He and Father were soon deep in a political discussion. Sally noticed that Mother and Grandmother, far from being bored as ladies generally were at such things, listened with painful interest.

"If what you say is true, Mr. Dorsey," Grandmother said, "I dread to think of these children journeying into the wilderness."

"Oh, it's all too true, Mistress Murray, ma'am," Mr. Dorsey assured her, passing his plate for more hominy. "The people are flocking back into Frederick Town from the whole western frontier. If you thought the trouble with the Indians ended when the war was over, you were vastly mistaken."

"If it's as bad as all that, sir," Father argued, "why do men of substance in Philadelphia, like Dr. Franklin, for example, urge men to pull up stakes and strike out for the western lands?"

"With all due respect to Dr. Franklin, sir, you people in Pennsylvania have ever been too trusting of the tribes," said Mr. Dorsey.

"Tush, sir," Grandmother put in, "when have Maryland folks had Indian trouble?"

"You've heard of Tom Cresap, ma'am?"

"Oh, to be sure, but he was off in the mountains, back of the Conococheague, or whatever its barbarous name is. The Calverts as well as the Penns have ever been gentle-dealing with the Indians."

"These aren't your nice, peaceable, fishing Indians, ma'am. These aren't Nanticokes and Piscataways. These are the Shawnees and the Mingoes. They're lifting scalps from the Lakes to the Smokies and all because of that red devil, Pontiac!"

"Who is Pontiac, sir?" Sally asked. She was half in and half out of the dining room door. There was a real, spotted, shaggy-necked pony waiting with Dilsy's James at the bridle, but the strange, ringing name caught her ear.

"Pontiac, young missy, is a chief of the Ottawa tribe. He led the warriors who killed that nincompoop, Braddock, I'm told. And now he has hatched a fantastic scheme for uniting all the tribes in the western lands to drive the settlers back—into the sea, he hopes!"

"And what did this Cresap, whoever he may be, do?" Father asked, as Sally's mouth made a round O of astonishment.

"You don't know Tom Cresap, sir? I'm astonished at you! It's you Pennsylvanians who are his hate and abomination! He thinks you have reft a great wedge of the state of Maryland away under false pretenses. He claims that Philadelphia itself should be in the state of Maryland, if the Calverts had their rights!"

"What says Governor Sharpe to all this?"

"Oh, he hems and haws—little it matters to him, though he has sent out powder and ball to the western settlements."

"To protect them from the Penns or the Indians?"

"You jest, sir! But seriously, the Cresaps have been a tower of strength on the western borders. Do you know, sir, that they have built stone houses like unto forts, for defense against the savages? With a spring flowing under the house, lest they be cut off from water during an attack!"

"That is a smart idea," Grandmother Murray approved.

"All you say is no doubt very true, sir," Father said, "but surely this Pontiac can be no threat for any length of time."

"He's a wily one, Master Redpath. And, I must admit, the Cresaps have helped foment the trouble. So enraged were they over the slaying of the settlers, that they turned around and massacred a whole village of the Shawnees, and it turned out that some of them had been good Christians and well-disposed to the whites. Logan, the good chief, was one of the slain. Well, 'twas too bad, but I insist, sir, this is no time to take a woman and child into the western country!"

Sally waited to hear no more. It was too much like the

chatter of the girls at Miss Collingwood's when she told them about her trip. Dilsy's James helped her up on the pony and trotted beside her as she rode. She spent a wonderful morning, seeing wide fields of tobacco, wheat ripening under the spring sun, cows grazing in placid meadows along Jones' Falls. Mother and Father cantered briskly after them a little later, and even Grandmother Murray, businesslike in a wide straw hat and brown riding habit, followed on a gray mare to look over her acres.

"I'm amazed at the wheat, Mother," Matilda Redpath said. " 'Twas all tobacco up to now, was it not?"

"Aye, the neighbors call me a doddering old fool," said Grandmother, gaily. "But I tell them wheat will make me rich when their land is all leached out from this pestilent sotweed, tobacco! If the Carrolls over on Doughoregan Manor can put in wheat for Mr. Ellicott's Mills up above the Elk Ridge Landing, so can Amelia Murray!"

The next day was Sunday. It was to be the Redpaths' last day at Murray's Range, for Father was impatient to get on with their journey, and he disliked keeping Jacob Stoltzfus idle. It was a sober procession that wound its way back into Baltimore Town in time for service at St. Paul's. The Redpaths filed into the Murray pew under the curious eyes of the congregation. Mother's old friends had had little notice of her visit, except for what the slaves on horseback could give, dropping messages at the Stevensons' and Smiths' and other estates around the hills above the Town. Sally had to be restrained from taking Lady Georgeanna to church. She had been swathed in her silk coverings long enough, Sally felt, and deserved more of an airing than her exhibition to Dilsy's young ones gave her.

The service progressed without incident, and Sally was nodding drowsily on her knees, her prayer book propped on the pew ahead, when the rector's faintly singsong intonation changed into a perfectly normal voice and he announced, "Let us pray for those among us who may need the direct help of the Almighty and the prayers of this congregation.

"Oh Lord, we beseech Thee to look down on Thy servant, Perry Bradshaw, master of the schooner *Isabel,* who is long overdue from Jamaica. Protect him from pirates and hurricanes, though it is not yet the season, Lord, and comfort his spouse, Esther, who is brought to bed of a fine little boy. Grant that the deep shall give up its secrets. Amen."

"Amen," whispered Sally, suddenly feeling very close to Mistress Bradshaw. She seemed to see her in a vast four-poster, in a tiny room overlooking the harbor, a new baby in her arms, and a terrible emptiness in the little house with its steep red roof.

But the rector was speaking again. "Oh, Lord, we beseech Thee to take under Thy sheltering wing a family whose mother was christened in this church. They are journeying into the wilderness, oh God, in the face of the savages. Protect them from Thy red children who have not learned to honor Thee. Keep the Redpaths, Henry, Matilda and Sarah, in the hollow of Thy hand. Grant them safe return and comfort the loved ones left behind. Amen."

Sally felt very small and humble and a little embarrassed, especially when people came up to the Redpath family after the service and patted her head and shook their own heads sadly. She blushed up to the roots of her hair when the rector blessed her after communion.

A wonderful afternoon followed for Sally. She spent it playing with her Murray cousins and Dilsy's younger children on the wide front lawn, while neighbors rode and drove in and out, and ladies and gentlemen overflowed the porch and sat on the grass under the mulberry trees. Sally was constantly summoned to curtsey to the people who had known her mother as a little girl. She displayed Lady Georgeanna to a most appreciative audience, too. The ladies had not seen very many fashion dolls of late— the local captains were too busy catching up on the tobacco trade and carrying flour to the West India Islands. It was whispered about that a number of Baltimore folks had had no heart for the war with France and had gone on selling flour to the French in the Indies, right under the noses of King George's navy!

Then there was supper, with fresh-caught shad from the Bay, and bowls of new strawberries and rich country cream. When Sally went to bed, she could hear Mother and Grandmother in low conversation in the next room. They talked for hours, and Sally knew that they were trying to make up for four years' absence before a parting that might well be forever.

The next morning, they all rode into town together right after breakfast. The first thing that met their eyes was Jacob Stoltzfus, standing foursquare in front of the *Indian Queen,* his broad felt hat on the back of his head. He was deep in conversation with a group of other wagoners.

"Good news, Herr Redpath!" he called. "Ve did vell in

coming here. I haf contracted to take seffen more vagons to Fort Pitt!"

Mother did not say anything, but she nodded merrily at Father's wry face. Her whim had paid off for Jacob!

The caravan set forth in another hour. The parting with Grandmother Murray was tearful, and caused many onlookers to wipe their eyes. A wagonload of country folk who came clattering in from the western road stared at the party in angry disbelief.

"Goin' *west*? Air you-all daft? We done left Hager's on the Conococheague. Rachel's even goin' back to England!"

"You may stay in this bloodstained wilderness," a young woman in a travel-stained dress and a drooping cap sobbed, "but you were born here! I'm taking the first ship back to Bristol."

"Aye, you were born here!" Father said, striding over to the battered wagon. "This is your land you're leaving, man. Are you letting a few measly savages fright you?"

"Mister, I don't know who you be," the driver of the wagon said, "but the measly savages kin have it. You ain't never heard no war whoop, hev ye?"

Father looked from Jacob, stolid and expressionless, to Madam Murray, silently wiping her eyes on an embroidered handkerchief. The bystanders shuffled their feet and shrugged their shoulders. The town was full of refugees. Somebody actually going west, determined to settle, must either be very brave or terribly foolish.

"What have you got in those wagons you're convoying, Jacob?" Father asked.

"Flour," Jacob answered, calmly mounting the lazy-board of the leading Conestoga, "molasses, nails—und gunpowder."

The long whip curled and slashed the air, uncoiling with a crack like a gunshot.

"Farewell! Farewell, and God be with you!" cried Madam Murray, and all the watchers yelled good-bye as though they were seeing the wagons off for another planet.

"Good-bye," Sally called, and because the tears filled her eyes, Grandmother Murray swam in a mist that did not clear until she became a small, dark figure, standing between Abram and James in the inn yard, far behind the caravan that was beginning to climb the first long hill to the west.

CHAPTER 3

LADY GEORGEANNA GOES A-VOYAGING

Lady Georgeanna sat stiff and proud in Sally Redpath's lap. Her sweeping satin hat, crowned with actual plumes, was perched jauntily above a wig of real hair, curled elaborately. Her waxen face was tinted to resemble that of a lady of fashion, even to the tiny patch just above the corner of her mouth. Her bodice was fitted to her wooden body without a wrinkle. It was made of cherry satin, trimmed with the finest and most delicate of French lace. Her skirts belled out over no less than four petticoats, edged with more lace. Her wooden legs wore silk stockings. Her absurdly tiny wooden feet were shod in black velvet slippers with square-cut buckles on the toes. And, joy to behold, they were protected from wet weather by a little pair of pattens, carved from wood and painted yellow, tied on with yellow ribbons. She wore an overskirt of cherry satin, lined with white, turned back to show an outer petticoat of wonderfully pleated paduasoy. Where the overskirt was caught up, tiny clusters of real silk roses were fastened with loops of black velvet. Her ridiculous little hands were gloved in white kid.

It was a tribute to Sally's care that the doll's costume had remained almost as good as new throughout the journey. Every night she brushed the dust of the road from the satin flounces, curled the tiny plumes over her finger, and settled the curls of the wig. Then she wrapped Lady Georgeanna in a large square of cream-colored India silk and laid her carefully at the foot of the bed. If it was an inn bed, she covered her completely with Mother's cloak, lest some light-fingered fellow traveler be tempted to investigate such a promising bundle. To have Lady Georgeanna stolen would be as bad as losing a child to the Indians, Sally felt.

The possession of Lady Georgeanna had given Sally great prestige among the girls of Miss Collingwood's establishment. The younger ones loved her just because she was a doll such as they had never seen before. The older girls admired her because she was what she was—not a toy at all, but a fashion doll from London.

When the fine ladies of New York and Philadelphia and Baltimore wanted to buy a new gown, they had no fashion books or papers to show them the latest styles. Unless they ordered a dress from some great dressmaker in London or Paris and waited months for a ship to carry the letter, and months more for another ship to fetch home the gown, through storms and pirates and blockades, they had to rely on the fashion dolls. The ladies of Philadelphia would drive to the establishment of Madame Finch in Broad

Street and, while their carriages waited outside, settle down with a great rustling of skirts. Sally had been there with her mother once and thought it was very exciting to see the handsome costumes and the fine cloaks and furs. Sally and her mother were nicely dressed, to be sure—Sally had a real India lawn gown, that spring, and a bonnet with flowers, and Mrs. Redpath wore her silk shawl and the wonderful green hat with the plumes. But some of the merchants' wives and the ladies of quality from the Governor's circle dazzled the eye with their silks and satins and brocades, their ropes of pearls and powdered hair with plumes and flowers worked into the braids and curls.

Then Madame Finch, part French and a born actress, swept in wearing a gray damask morning-gown and Brussels lace cap and followed by a small Negro boy in turban and sash. He carried an enormous red cushion, on which was standing the first of a series of dolls. How the ladies squealed and whispered behind their French fans! Such a nodding of feathers and bobbing of artificial flowers! The little boy, addressed as Selim (his name was Jeremiah, but Selim sounded so Turkish and fashionable, Madame thought), carried the dolls one after another, slowly around the circle of ladies. As he went, he turned slowly about, so all could see every detail of the doll's costume.

"La, Amelia, hair is going to be plainer this year," a stout lady with a tremendous tower of powdered hair decorated with stuffed birds, exclaimed.

"And see how the pearls are worked right into the pattern on the brocade. Madame Finch, I must have a gown just like that for the Assembly Ball!" another cried.

"Just arrived on the *Belle Aurore* from Dunkerque,"

Madame purred. "Not two months from Paris, *mesdames,* the latest word."

After the dolls had been paraded and exclaimed over, little Selim staggered in under bolt after bolt of marvelous cloth. Damask and paduasoy, lutestring and India mull, lawns and cassimeres and satins, in such colors and patterns! Sally's mouth watered at the very sight of them.

And so it went, until dusk began to fall and Selim's female counterpart, a tiny girl called Zelie, brought in tea and little cakes for the ladies. Madame Finch took orders, arranged fittings, flattered stout ladies and cajoled timid ones. But Sally, even with her mouth full of seedcake, had eyes only for the dolls. Time after time, her longing gaze went back to the one in cherry-colored satin. Madame, who noticed that gaze, remembered it, along with a thousand details of design and color.

A little while before the Redpaths left Philadelphia, Sally and her mother went to Madame Finch's shop to settle their bill. Madame was horrified, so she said, at the long and dangerous journey ahead for them. Who knew what scalpings and burnings they would have to endure at the hands of the Indians? Madame, being part French, diplomatically left out any reference to French Indians or English Indians. She held up her hands in despair.

"The men, it is all their fault. If we women had our way, there would be no fighting over who settled the Ohio. Let *La Belle Rivière* belong to King Louis or King George. Just let them settle the fur trade and stop the blockade on the seas, and everybody will be happy, no?"

Then she clapped her plump hands together. Little

Selim, minus his green turban, but wearing a scarlet jacket and white Turkish trousers, bobbed in. She whispered to him. The child ran out, grinning. Presently he returned, carrying something wrapped in a piece of creamy silk material. Madame took it from him and placed it on Sally's knees.

"Just a little remembrance from old Madame, who had no little girls to play with dolls."

Sally, scarcely daring to breathe, unwrapped the folds of silk. There, complete from bonnet to pattens, was the doll in cherry-colored satin.

Sally could not speak. She wanted to laugh and cry all at once. Never, never had she dreamed of this.

"Is—is she really mine?" the words struggled to her lips at last.

"All yours, *chérie*. I saw how you loved her the other day at the showing. Since you will be wearing homespun and moccasins when your fine clothes from Madame Finch are all worn out, keep her to remind you of what you have come from." Madame and Matilda Redpath exchanged glances. "There will be no fine clothes on *La Belle Rivière*. Some day, you will want to be beautiful for some one. Maybe you will be clever with the needle, *N'est ce pas?* You can make over one of your *maman's* dresses after this one. No one knows anything about styles in the wilderness. You will be the belle of them all."

Sally had tried to thank Madame, then, but she couldn't seem to find her tongue. But her mother and Madame had understood. When Sally carried the doll out to the carriage, old Caesar handed them in most carefully. He knew valuable stuff when he saw it.

Sally had been allowed to take the doll to school with her just once. Oddly enough, Miss Collingwood did not seem to mind the interruption to discipline and decorum. The girls crowded around with cries of admiration, but Miss Collingwood, whose gowns were all of the period of King George I, was more interested than anyone.

"Paris is ever the center of culture, I fear," she murmured, fingering the satin overskirts lovingly. The girls did not know just what she meant, but they sensed that the old eagle was in an unusual mood.

"What will you call her, Sally?"

"Lud," said Kitty Fairfax, whose uncle owned half the land in Virginia, "she should have a French name, since she's from Paris."

Sally never hesitated. Her father's politics had seldom crossed her mind, but she had heard him, along with the other gentlemen in the library at home, toasting the royal family at New Year's. Surely Georgeanna and Caroline were fine names, and they were associated with the royal family. A French name would be pretty—Madame Finch was named Lucille Marie for her French mother—but in these times, an English one seemed safer.

"Georgeanna because of King George, and Caroline for his mother," Sally said. "But I can't think of an elegant last name."

She had puzzled over that last name for nearly a week. It came to her one day while she was listening to her mother reading a novel aloud. It was way over her head, being about high life in London. People were always fighting duels and falling in love in the silliest way. Why anybody wasted time on such stuff, Sally could not think. She liked Madame Perrault's fairy tales much better. But there was a name that kept coming out in the reading that fascinated her. Lord Maltravers, it was. Maltravers leapt on his horse and galloped off in search of the Marchioness. Maltravers ran Sir Hubert through with his Italian rapier. Maltravers rescued the gipsy and found his fortune. A most elegant name! And so, Lady Georgeanna Caroline became Lady Georgeanna Caroline Maltravers.

And now, here was Lady Georgeanna Caroline Maltravers riding through the Blue Ridge Mountains toward Fort Pitt. She had no riding habit or homespun gown. She rode in satin splendor in Sally's arms, beside Jacob Stoltzfus from Lancaster. If she minded the jolting of the wagon, she gave no sign. Like a truly high born lady, she made no complaint; not even when the warm spring sun shone too long upon her dainty wax nose. Before Sally noticed this, the tip of Lady Georgeanna's delicate nose had run a trifle. It looked lopsided! Alarmed, Sally pinched at it gently, to get it back in shape. She must remember not to hold her ladyship in the bright sunlight any more. She got a calico rag from her mother and spread it over the doll's bonnet like a canopy. Thus protected, Lady Georgeanna rode serenely toward Fort Cumberland.

Neither Sally nor her beloved waxen friend could have guessed what lay ahead on the road over the mountains. Sally's father had told her how General Braddock had had the road carved out of the endless forest, all the way from Fort Cumberland in Maryland to the Monongahela River. Some people said the general didn't care a rap about whether the army had a road to march on, but he needed a road for his fine carriage. Couldn't ride a horse across the mountains. Had to have all the comforts of home. Wouldn't travel in a wagon. Too undignified! Well, the general was where carriages and wagons didn't matter, now. Out yonder on the mountains, he was, buried far from the dress parades and drills that were his idea of warfare. Nobody had told the Indians about that kind of fighting. They hid behind the trees and shot at the soldiers. General Braddock thought men ought to be marched onto a battlefield in neat rows, to shoot at each other in polite order. Well, he knew better now!

If it hadn't been for some of our brave woodsmen and hunters, with those long Lancaster rifles, hiding behind the trees like the Indians, there would have been no soldiers left alive to tell the tale. It didn't take the Highlanders long to catch on. Back home in Scotland they had hidden behind rocks and down in the heather to shoot at those same redcoats they were helping now. They could fight Indian fashion, too. But a man in a bright red coat, marched in formation through the dark woods—he never had a chance. All this Sally heard from her father and the men on the wagons.

As the bells rang merrily on, and the wagons jolted along beside the swift, blue river called Potomac, Sally began to feel little shivers go up and down her spine. Cabins were farther and farther apart now. Except for the road, muddy and rutted from the wheels of the wagons, the whole world seemed to wear a cloak of green leaves. That even covered the long spines of the hills. When the wind blew, you could see the ripple coming over the far-off treetops, just like it came across the wheat fields back beyond Frederick Town, where there were lots of farms settled. Way up in the sky, hawks and buzzards circled lazily. A couple of times, Sally caught the white flick of a deer's tail, as a slim, brown shape bounded into the trees. Once Jacob Stoltzfus nudged her as she dozed in the sunshine. A beautiful little red fox lay stretched out on a warm rock beside the trail, his bright eyes watching them without fear.

"*Reinich der Fuchs,*" Jacob said with a smile. "He lives everywhere."

It was on just such a sunny afternoon that the Redpath party met the Tatums. The wagons were creaking up the long slopes of Sideling Hill. Far above, the wooden ridge seemed to lie like a wall between them and the West. Behind them lay the pleasant valley of Tonolloway Creek. The safely stockaded parade ground of little Fort Frederick was behind them, too. They had passed two days there, resting the horses and mending gear. Sally had played with the children of the garrison. The boys had wanted to play soldiers and Indians, of course, only letting the girls into the game because they could scream so well during the "Indian attack." Sally had screamed very well, indeed, and was scalped by a Shawnee brave whose hair was strangely yellow for an Indian. His war paint was mostly brick dust and bear's grease, and he wore a large owl's feather in his headband. His name was Robert Jessup.

This sunny afternoon, Sally had scrambled down from the wagon. She was walking beside it, making as good time as the horses up the steep grade. Jacob was on the other side, at Brown Girl's head, his long whip in his hand.

The road disappeared around a sharp bend and came out again beyond a clump of trees. The Tatums were around this bend, coming downhill and appearing as if by magic out of the woods.

There were four of them. First came a man. He was a little, skinny fellow with a matted beard, in greasy buckskins. He wore a battered felt hat covered with dark stains, partly hiding a layer of bandages. They were still fairly clean. He was leading a broken-down horse by a rope bridle. On its saggy back a scrawny woman rode. Her faded linsey-woolsey dress clung to her bony body. Various bundles and boxes were roped on behind her. Following the horse, a half-grown boy stumbled along with an enormous pack on his back. It seemed to be bedding and small household stuff. At his side walked a girl Sally's age. It was at her that Sally stared. She had stringy yellow hair—almost white, it was so pale—and huge blue eyes that seemed to be looking right through Sally. She was wearing the dirtiest rag of a dress Sally had ever seen, and her moccasins were worn through to the ground. On her back was a pitiful little pack of odds and ends.

The wagons came to a halt. The horses were winded anyhow, and the drivers plodded up one by one to stand and swap conversation. Sally's father joined them, still looking strange in his buckskins, to his daughter, who was used to him in his Philadelphia broadcloth and embroidered small-clothes. Mrs. Redpath, stretching her legs from her long afternoon's ride, came up to her husband.

"Bound fer Cumberland?" the little man asked. His voice had a queer whiney drawl. "Ah was too, onct.

Name's Tatum. Now Ah'm goin' home to James River Hundred. All burnt out. Ever'thin' gone."

"Injuns?"

"Shawnees an' Delawahs. Done burnt mah cabin an' sculpit me. Lef' me fo' daid. Elvirah she done hid with the chillun in a holla' tree. We ain't nevah gwine leave the settlemints no mo'.''

The men of the wagon train asked questions. Matilda Redpath tried to talk to the gaunt woman, who answered in a faint, tight voice. She was too worn-out and miserable to cry any more. Their cabin had been somewhere in the jumble of hills beyond the Youghiogheny River. The raiding party had burned the cabin. When the Indians had gone, Mrs. Tatum had waited a whole day and night in the hollow tree with little Nannie. The boy, Willum, had sneaked back to the charred ruin and found his father lying in the path with his scalp torn away. He had called his mother then. She had fixed up Tatum the best she knew how, and the three of them had managed to get him to the shelter of Fort Burd. They had found the horse, they said. Nobody asked them where. The few belongings they had rescued from the burning were on its back, and on their own.

"Why go all the way back to Tidewater?" asked Henry Redpath. "There's plenty good land in Maryland, just east of South Mountain."

"Ah'm a James Rivah Hundred man," Tatum said sadly, "and Ah should nevah have crossed them mountains. Ah'll go back an' scratch terbaccah on James Rivah till Ah die."

Sally tried to get the girl, Nannie, to come and sit in

her father's wagon for a few minutes. Nannie just smiled a faraway smile and said nothing. Matilda Redpath was hurrying to bundle together a few clothes she could spare. "I can't bear to think of that woman in that one poor dress," she said. "And that child's almost bone bare." When Sally got back to the Stoltzfus wagon, she found Nannie Tatum standing there, just staring up at the lazyboard.

Lady Georgeanna Caroline Maltravers sat on the seat in all her satin glory, smiling her painted smile at the wilderness. And Nannie Tatum looked at her with the eyes of a child who had just seen into heaven.

"Isn't she a love? She's mine," Sally said proudly. And then, because Nannie looked the way she did, she scrambled up as Jacob had taught her and handed Lady Georgeanna down.

"Go on, hold her," she urged. The hands that Nannie stretched longingly toward the doll were black dirty, with grimy, broken nails and streaked knuckles. Then, because even Nannie Tatum knew what was the right thing to do, she dropped them back to her sides.

"Ah'm too raddled. Ah'd spile huh."

Sally stood as close to Nannie as she dared—her mother had whispered that it was wiser not to get too close to folks who hadn't had a wash in so long—and showed her all Lady Georgeanna's clothes. She told her how the doll had come over the sea on a ship from France.

Nannie's face puckered. "Pa says it was the French what set the redsticks on us," she whispered.

Sally skipped the rest of the story. She just made the doll lift her arms and move her stiff, wooden legs as if she were dancing. She walked her along the ground as though she were a baby learning to step. Nannie Tatum followed along, quivering with love and longing.

"Ah had a poppet, too. It was a wooden one. Pa made a face on it wi' charcoal, an' Ma she made it a gown outen stroudin' cloth. Reckon she got burnt up in the cabin. She was my onliest baby."

"What did you call her?" Sally asked.

"Silly."

"Silly?"

"Aye, Silly folks make you feel like singin'. When Ah had Silly to rock, Ah never felt lonesome. Ah'd sing hymn tunes to huh all day long."

Sally kept on showing Lady Georgeanna's charms, and presently Nannie Tatum was talking more and more. She told Sally about helping Ma dress the skins of the deer Pa killed with his rifle gun, to make moccasins and shirts. She told of the long winters with the mountains deep in snow. She even told about how scared she had been, crouched in the hollow tree with Ma, while the painted Indians yipped and danced in the firelight from the burning cabin. It was as if, once started, she had to pour out the terror that had been choked down inside her all that time.

Meanwhile, Mrs. Redpath had pressed the bundle of small comforts upon Mrs. Tatum. The woman was proud. At first, she did not want to take the things, but the sight of the soap had been too much for her. Sally remembered Callie pouring the soap back home in Philadelphia, with her mother supervising. No lady was too fine to do such things, she always said. As a girl on her father's manor outside of Baltimore Town, she had learned soapmaking from Grandmother Murray.

Mrs. Tatum looked at that soap. She looked down at her soiled gown and dirty hands. Her face worked.

"Ah'm everlastingly obliged to ye, ma'am," she said.

A short time later, the Tatums emerged from the woods at the roadside. A spring, bubbling and gurgling within earshot, had joined forces with the soap to take the worst of the caked dirt from faces and hands. Cold water and lye soap are not the best cleansers, but they had worked wonders. When Mrs. Tatum could pause long enough in her journey to heat water in her iron pot, the family might know a real scrubbing. But now, you could tell what color they were. And Nannie timidly put out her red-knuckled little hands to Lady Georgeanna.

"Now Ah kin tech huh," she whispered.

Sally placed the doll gently in her arms.

"Kin Ah dandle huh jest a mite, Sally?"

Sally nodded. Bearded teamsters, muttering in Pennsylvania German, stood around waiting to resume the march. The Redpaths were ready to push on. But somehow, they felt like letting Nannie Tatum hold that doll. It might help to make up for the awful thing that had happened back there on the Youghiogheny.

Nannie rocked back and forth by the roadside, the doll in her arms, alone in the whole world with her baby. Jacob Stoltzfus raised his whip, let it unfurl itself along the red earth with a resounding crack. Brown Girl and Dopple, Leibchen and Grayling, Hans and Dunder, gathered their big shoulders together and bent their heads to the pull. With a jangle of bells, the first wagon moved off, slowly straining up the slope of Sideling Hill. The second followed, then the third.

"Come, child," said Matilda Redpath softly. "Get your poppet and be ready to mount the wagon when it passes."

Sally looked at Nannie Tatum. The strangest feeling was growing inside her. Lady Georgeanna was her beloved doll. Madame had wanted her to have her, to remind her of home, in the wilderness, to make her a great lady when she grew up. But there was more to being a great lady than wearing cherry-colored satin gowns. Never, never could she forget Madame Finch and her kindness. But never, never could she forget that Nannie Tatum's onliest baby had been lost in the fire back there across the mountains. If she did this kind deed, she would feel the good of it in her heart forever. Somebody else seemed to be pushing her across the road to Nannie. She stood beside the absorbed little girl and touched her gently on the arm.

"Let me have her a minute," she whispered. Nannie came out of her dream with a small sigh. She gave Lady Georgeanna one long hug, then handed her back to her owner. Sally held her doll tightly, her eyes shut. She felt the beautiful satin dress with loving hands. Maybe some day, if she was good enough and said her prayers every night, she would have a lovely doll like this again. Then she pushed Lady Georgeanna back at the startled child.

"Take her. She's yours," she sobbed, and turned to run to her father, who was coming up with the wagon. Without a word, she clung to him. He looked at her, tears running down her face. He looked at Nannie Tatum, clutching the doll to her thin body, half hidden by the

Never could she forget that Nannie Tatum's onliest baby had been lost back there across the mountains.

billowing satin skirts. Matilda Redpath met them both at the turn in the road. No one said anything.

As the wagon groaned upgrade around the bend, the Tatum family still stood beside the scrawny horse, staring uphill. Nannie held Lady Georgeanna high in her arms.

"Good-bye! Good-bye! God bless ye!" She called.

Lady Georgeanna disappeared from view. She was on her way back to Tidewater. Ahead lay the wilderness.

CHAPTER

BEARS IN THE BERRY PATCH

For some time, the men in the wagon train had been whispering together and casting suspicious glances at the wooded mountainsides. They had left Fort Cumberland behind, pushing up the narrow trace toward Fort Pitt. The road was awful beyond Fort Cumberland. Sometimes the trees closed in almost to the trail side. This made everyone uneasy. It was an ideal place for an ambush, truce or no truce. Sometimes the trail went right through a swamp. "Glades," they called them, up here. Back when the road had been built, logs had been put across the worst places so that wagons would not get bogged down. It might have been a good road, Henry Redpath told Sally and her mother one noonday while they were resting the horses, only nobody would listen to Colonel Washington. Sally had heard about him. He was the man from Virginia that Kitty Fairfax used to talk about at Miss Collingwood's. He had been with General Braddock when he was killed. Colonel Washington believed in fighting from behind trees, like the Indians. The redsticks respected him, too. Called him "Big Hand."

Well, Father said, this Colonel Washington had wanted the road out of Maryland and Virginia to be the main highway over the mountains from the settlements, but it went only as far as the spot where the battle had been. It stopped seventeen miles from Fort Pitt. The big road, the one from Philadelphia, went straight through to Fort Pitt. Now that he saw how bad this road was getting, Father was sorry that he had freighted all his goods down the Bay to Baltimore, instead of going on west through Carlisle. Of course, it meant that his wife had been able to pay a last visit to her mother on the big farm outside of Baltimore Town and Sally had had a wonderful time there. Also, Jacob Stoltzfus had made a few profitable pounds freighting a load of chairs into Baltimore in one of his wagons. But alas—the Baltimore Pike was fine until you got to Fort Cumberland. Now it was a mudhole, a bog, a scratch in the forest. The road from Braddock's Defeat up to the Forbes Road was a mere trace. They'd be lucky to get the wagons through. And here, on top of everything, Indian sign!

The wagon train had taken on a guide at Fort Cumberland. He was a queer, silent man, who looked more like an Indian than a white man. He wore stained and patched-up buckskins and had his hair hanging in a greasy scalp lock. His Lancaster gun was the longest Sally had ever seen. It was inlaid with beautiful brass trimmings, and on the patch box was engraved his name, Adam Byles, in curling script. The trigger guard had a running vine engraved on it, ending in a cluster of grapes. The butt of the gun was bound in brass and decorated with a flying goose. Adam called his gun Shawnee Stopper. Sally had begged him to let her hold it, just once. Adam Byles was a sour, silent man. He was outraged with Henry Redpath for bringing a woman and a girl-child into the wilderness. He was angry with them for being there. But when he heard how Sally had given her beloved doll to the Tatum child, he softened. "That were a kindly-meant thing," he said. And on the morning that Adam Byles found Indian sign, he let Sally hold the long rifle. Of course, she could hardly lift it enough to sight along it. The men laughed at her, staggering around as she tried to bring it up to eye level. Then Adam had come behind her and knelt down. He steadied the long barrel for her, resting it over a log as she braced herself against his hard chest. Sally liked the queer little man, even if he did smell so much like an animal. He showed her how to squint through the sights at her imaginary target. "Keep her steady, so," he whispered, "and niver shoot till ye see what ye're aimin' fer right in them sights."

Then he had actually sat down beside the trail—Jacob Stoltzfus and one of the wagoners were mending a broken trace—and showed her how to load and prime.

He measured a charge of black powder from his powder horn that was covered with hearts and tulip-flowers carved by some German artist in the green valley above Lebanon. Next, he delved in the brass patch box and took out a bit of rag which he spat on. Having poured the powder carefully down the long, thin barrel, he wrapped the wet rag around a ball which he produced from a small buckskin bag. Then he took the long hickory ramrod and drove the wrapped ball down the barrel. Holding the gun across his flat stomach, he took the powder horn in his right hand and dribbled a few grains against the flint, behind the big steel trigger. Then he knelt down with the gun barrel resting on a stump and took aim with as much care as if a Shawnee warrior were outlined in those sights. He screwed his face into an agony of concentration and pulled the trigger. A hundred and fifty yards away, a pine cone dropped from a tree that was only a green blob to Sally.

When the wagon train got under way again, Adam was riding his little red mare half a mile ahead. They were in a small valley between two hills. He was almost out of sight, up the farther hill. Sally, riding with Jacob in the first wagon, saw Adam Byles pull the mare to a stop. He dismounted and picked up something from the road. Then he leaped into the saddle again, turned his mare's head and trotted downhill to meet the train. The men got down off the wagons and crowded around him. Sally ducked under their arms and squirmed her way as close to him as she could.

"See thet?" Adam was holding something in the palm of his hand. It was just a curious trinket of beads and copper as far as Sally could see, but it meant more to Adam.

"Shawnee," he said, and the listeners shivered.

All that day and the morning of the next—after an uneasy night full of sounds that filled Sally's dreams with painted warriors—the wagons creaked along. The woods seemed full of eyes. Sally's neck crept at the thought. A peace treaty sounded so safe and binding in quiet Philadelphia, so definite in stockaded forts with rangers on the ramparts. Here, in the green quiet of the woods, it became

And on the morning that Adam Byles found Indian sign, he let Sally hold the long rifle.

only words on a piece of parchment. How much did it mean to the Indians with the arrows and stolen English muskets, behind the trees? It would be so easy to pick off a lonely train of wagons, then melt away over the mountains and be gone. The soldiers were very far off. Nobody in the forests would tell.

Sally had no desire to leave the group of whispering people until the noontime rest was nearly over. She had been properly meek when she had listened to Adam's warning about sticking close to camp and wagons, but she was bored stiff now, after the fifth re-telling of how Henricus Zentz had met the Ottawa war party at the fords of the Monongahela last May a year ago, and what he had said, and they had done— There were berries on those bushes up yonder—fat, juicy blackberries! The jays were quiet in the trees on the mountain. That meant there was nothing up that way to frighten them. So Sally just took the little pail and slipped into the bushes. She could pick it full and be back before Reimersdoffer got his axles greased. The fresh berries would be a nice treat for her mother.

The sun was hot on the hillside as Sally scrambled up over the rocks. Years ago, lightning had struck here and started a forest fire. The burned, black trunks stood like sticks of charcoal among the tall fireweed and ferns. A hawk circled lazily overhead. Everything was still, except for a jay scolding on a branch. His outburst startled Sally until she realized he was scolding *her*. Now, here the berry bushes were really thick. Why, they weren't blackberries like the few scattered bushes downhill, but blueberries! Lovers of barren meadows and burned-over lands, the sturdy bushes carpeted the ground, laden with plump, shiny fruit. Sally picked and ate, ate and picked, until her pail was nearly full. How surprised Mother would be when she saw the blueberries! Sally sat down for a minute on a big, flat rock and looked about her. To the west, the mountains wore that dark, shiny green that they get in hot weather. These were the near-by hills—the far-away ones were all faint and hazy with the heat. Sally pushed back her hat and fanned herself with her apron. Suddenly, from just over the ridge, there came the funniest sounds! It seemed as though someone were talking, someone who was scolding a child. Funny little whimpers and snarls and squeals were all mixed in with it, and every now and then it sounded like somebody calling. Sally felt a little frightened.

Then a cool puff of wind struck her hot face. She looked up to see a big, black thundercloud swelling like an enormous castle over the hill. And at the same time, she realized that she was lost. The whole side of the rocky hill looked the same. She could see no break in the green bushes below at the edge of the burned place, where there should have been a little trail that she had made when she came through from the road. Sally sprang to her feet. For the first time since she had left the wagon train, she was really afraid. Father and Adam Byles had warned her, but she had known better than they. She had to be so smart. It was long past time for the wagons to move. They would be looking everywhere for her.

The snarling little noise over the hill grew louder. Worried as she was, Sally was so curious that she picked up her pail and started to climb the ridge. Just over the top, the fire had apparently burned itself out, for there were a few big trees growing unscorched amid the ferns and brush. And then Sally saw the bears!

Halfway up a little sapling, which shook under their weight, were two black bear cubs. At the bottom of another tree, a little bigger, stood a big mother bear, growling and grumbling and looking up into the branches. Sally was so startled that she dropped her pail. It hit the ground with a loud clank, spilling blueberries in all directions. Sally screamed, and the old bear wheeled around with a loud "whuff!" She looked at Sally, and Sally looked at her. At first Sally could not decide whether to run or try to climb a tree, but at last she made up her mind. She picked up the empty pail and banged it loudly.

The mother bear rumbled and growled like the thunder which was coming closer, but finally she dropped onto all fours and went lumbering off down the ridge in a scrambling hurry, leaving the cubs squealing in different keys from their tree.

Then suddenly, from the tree where the mother bear had been threatening, somebody called out in a curious language. Sally dropped the pail and stared up into the leaves. Two little feet in deerskin moccasins were digging into the bark. Two bright black eyes peered down at Sally in amazement. It was an Indian girl, no older than Sally herself!

"Oh, please come down!" Sally begged. She was so happy to see another child in the forest that she forgot about the old bear. The cubs, more afraid of the cuffing their mother would give them than of those queer two-legged animals, were backing down their tree. The Indian

Sally dropped the pail and stared up into the leaves. Two little feet in deerskin moccasins were digging into the bark.

girl came down cautiously, her black braids dangling. To Sally's surprise, there was a small boy, about three years old, up there with her. He was a fat little thing. The girl would swing herself down to a lower branch, reach up and help the little boy down, swing down again, and so on until she could drop to the ground. Then she held up her arms, and the boy threw himself into them, knocking her flat on her back. It was a hard bump, but neither child whimpered. They picked themselves up and looked at Sally.

"What's your name?" she asked.

The Indian girl giggled and said something in her funny talk. The little boy just stared. His mouth was purple from eating blueberries.

"Can't you talk any English at all?" Sally pleaded.

The girl seemed to understand the one word "English." She pointed to Sally solemnly and said, "Ingleese." Sally nodded in delight. The girl tapped Sally on her chest and kept repeating another word in her language. After a while Sally thought, maybe she's asking me my name. It wouldn't do any harm to guess at what she was saying. It was like a game. She pointed to herself and said loudly, "Sally. Sal-ly. My name is Sally."

The other girl laughed. She understood! She tapped Sally again and shouted, "Sal-ly! Sal-ly!" Sally nodded and laughed, too. The Indian girl poked herself and rattled off a mouthful of queer sounds. They must be her names, Sally guessed, trying to repeat them. The girl smiled and said them over and over. Soon the two were laughing like old friends, while the little boy stuffed himself with blueberries. He chattered a lot to himself, but would not let

Sally hug him. He was so sturdy and brown, she ached to hold him. The two girls went back to where Sally had dropped the pail. Both children scooped the spilled berries up and put them back, eating a good many more in the process.

The thunder was rumbling louder and louder. Sally looked up at the black sky in some dismay. She could never get back to the wagons before the storm broke, even if she knew the way. The Indian boy and girl looked at the clouds and jabbered excitedly. A bright, forked tongue of lightning flickered down the sky, followed by a shivering crack that seemed to shake the ground. The Indian girl seized Sally's hand and pulled her down the hillside. She led her first through some tall trees to an overhanging rock which made a shelter. The little boy ran after them, his hands still dripping berry juice. The three children crouched together under the big rock while the rain poured down.

Presently the Indian girl pulled up the deerskin bag which was fastened to the rawhide cord tied around her waist. This, with a tiny apron of skin, was all she wore besides her moccasins and some cheap blue glass beads. Sally watched while she took out something which she cradled in her arms. It was a doll, a poppet! Though it was small and crude compared to Lady Georgeanna Caroline Maltravers, the girl loved it so much! She rocked it and sang a little song to it. Sally put out her hand toward it timidly. She had never seen an Indian doll before. Presently the other girl, with a proud smile, held out the doll to Sally.

As Sally took it, she thought she had never seen a toy so queer. Its body was made of cornhusks, tightly wrapped and twisted together. Its face was painted with red and black, daubed on like an Indian's face decoration. It wore a small deerskin apron like the one the girl was wearing, and a tiny, white shell around its neck on a thread of wool that looked like it had been unraveled from a blanket. So the two girls played with the cornhusk doll while the thunderstorm lashed the forest outside. The little boy curled up like a puppy and slept.

The storm finally wore itself out, rumbling away over the mountains in the late afternoon. When the hot, bright sun made all the trees steam like teakettles, Sally and the Indian children came out of their shelter. Sally handed the doll back to the girl. She tried to make her understand that she must go now, although she hadn't the least idea which way. To her surprise, the little girl started off down the hill, looking back over her shoulder and beckoning. Sally followed because there was nothing else to do. Her skirts were torn with briars and soaked through from brushing the wet bushes. Mosquitoes buzzed and bit. Sally realized she must go downhill to get back to the wagons, for she had climbed all the way from the trail to the blueberries. So far, the Indian girl was right.

The little boy trotted along behind, making cross noises when he was left too far back in the bushes. Once, a covey of quail zoomed up from under their noses, scaring Sally half to death. Once, she nearly stumbled over a big box turtle lying in the grass. Quite suddenly, the Indian girl stopped short. She took Sally by the hand and spoke very earnestly in her strange language. She pointed off down

Sally thought she had never seen a toy so queer. Its body was made of cornhusks, tightly wrapped together.

the slope through some widely spaced trees. Sally looked and, sure enough, at the bottom of the hill she saw the red scar of the road. From far away, she could hear the voices of the teamsters and the jingle of the horse-bells. She threw her arms around the little girl and hugged her tightly.

"Oh, thank you, thank you!" Sally whispered. She took her new friend's hand to pull her along, but the girl drew back. She shook her head hard. Sally did manage to understand that she said, "No Ingleese," among the other things. She must be as afraid of white people as we are of redsticks, Sally realized. Then the little girl took her cornhusk doll from the pouch and pressed it into Sally's hands. With a quick, snatching movement, she took the pail of blueberries and dashed off up the hill. The boy-child squalled and followed.

Sally stood dazed, staring after them. "Come back! Oh, please come back!" she called, but the woods were suddenly as still as if no little girl and baby boy had ever raced away through the trees.

Five minutes later, Sally was being scolded in German and English by Jacob Stoltzfus, Adam Byles and her father. The wagons were lined up in the road. Some had already started on. Sally's mother was crying in the big Conestoga. Adam Byles, his rifle in his hand, had already searched the near-by woods. Some of the teamsters had threatened to go on without the Redpaths if they did not catch up by sunup the next day. Father was furious as well as frightened. Sally had given them all a bad afternoon.

Tearstained and repentant, Sally huddled in the wagon-bed, exiled from Jacob's lazy-board. Her mother sat silent and pale beside her. Her father sternly marched along near the wagon. Only the cornhusk doll remained to comfort her. Mother had been particularly cross about the missing pail. The only ray of light in the whole miserable evening dawned when Adam looked long at the doll.

" 'Twarn't a war party," he said, at length. "War parties don't tote childer with 'em. More'n likely 'twere Shawnee, come back to make medicine in the old fields."

So the train journeyed on with easier minds. And Sally held the cornhusk doll in her arms and wondered about the Indian children. Lady Georgeanna was going back to James River. The Shawnee poppet had come in her place. Sally wrapped the strange toy in her apron and crooned a lullaby as the wagon toiled westward.

CHAPTER

5

PRETTYING POLLY!

To Sally's surprise, after leaving Fort Pitt, there was another outpost of civilization hanging desperately on the edge of the wilderness. This was a combination of tavern, fort and jumping-off-place called Wicker's. The Redpaths and Adam Byle came up to it on the trace which struggled through the enclosing forest just at sunset.

Adam Byles spat into the bushes as he drew rein. "I'll stay by the wagon, Master Redpath," he growled. "Else they'll steal everything what ain't nailed down before mornin'. You, ma'am, had best carry any valuables on yore pusson, an' you, sir, keep a pistol handy an' wedge yore door shut."

"Save us, Master Byles," Mother said, peering anxiously at the sprawling log house in the gathering twilight, "if it's such a cutthroat place, why must we put up here at all?"

"Because ye've got a lame wheel hoss, fer one reason. Jacob Stoltzfus himself would tell ye to bide here, an' I aim to return this team an' wagon to him at Logstown in good shape." Adam was to see the Redpaths settled in on their claim before taking the Conestoga back to Fort Pitt, where Jacob would pick it up for the return journey to Philadelphia. They all missed the sturdy German wagoner. Father was no hostler, and Adam had his hands full with six big horses and his own red mare.

They drew up before Wicker's, and Adam led the hesitating procession into the shadowy common room of the tavern. A huge, red-faced woman in a dark red shortgown, her coarse black hair exploding stiffly from under a soiled mobcap, advanced to meet them, obviously surprised at such guests. Adam saluted her curtly. His sharp eyes roved over the grimy men at the fire, dismissed them as harmless for the time being.

"A very good evening to ye all, sir and madam and little missy," the woman purred, twisting her powerful hands in her grease-spotted apron. "I never looked to have such gentry in my house, or I'd have got the rooms redded up. I'm Ma Wicker. The house is yours, good people!" Then, raising her voice to a screech like a wildcat's, she yelled, "Poll! Poll Casselman! Ye good-fer-nuthin' huzzy, where are ye?"

The shadowy figure of a girl appeared at the back door of the room. "What d'ye want?"

"Git the best room redded up, afore I break every bone in yer wuthless body!"

The shadow ducked out of sight, and Ma Wicker advanced ominously on the men by the fire.

"Git up now, boys," she commanded. "Let these good folks have a warm."

"There's no need to do that, gentlemen," Father said

pleasantly. "It's a fine, warm evening, and we will be quite comfortable by the window."

Mother and Sally had already seated themselves on a long settle by the small window. It was covered with oiled paper and had heavy wooden shutters which could be bolted shut in the event of an attack. Of course, it let in no air, and the room was stuffy and warm.

"Hevn't I seed ye afore, somewheres?" Ma Wicker demanded of Adam Byles, who was standing near the door, leaning on his gun, so that he could keep an eye on the wagon.

"Thet ye have," he replied sourly. "Last March it was. I lost a good saddlebag that ye never were able to find. Would it be a miracle or an accident thet thet powder flask over yer mantel should have come out of thet same saddlebag?"

"Oh, to be sure now, I remember." The woman laughed, nervously, but with a sullen glare under her black brows. "I was a wonderin' who could ha' left it behind him. An' ye say it's yours? Can ye prove it, I wonder? Some o' the lads is awful light-fingered, I know, but I keeps a respectable house, I do."

Adam strode over to the huge mantel, plucked the powder flask off the wall and turned it over in his hand.

"My name bein' Adam Byles, an' this flask bein' scratched with the same on the horn, I reckon thet's proof enough." He thrust it into his deep pocket. "Now if the saddlebag's lyin' around loose, I'll be much obliged to have it back, too."

"Ye're welcome to look, I'm sure," the hostess snarled. "But ye make mighty free, Mister Byles."

"I don't like this place, Father," Sally whispered. "I don't like that woman, and it smells dreadful in here! Can't we sleep in the wagon tonight, please, Father?"

"Never mind, Sally," Mother whispered back. "I'm sure 'twill be all right."

"I'd advise us all to put a pleasant face on matters," said Father in a low voice. "Adam must bide with the wagon. He is right about this place, of course; but this is no region for lone camping out. Bear with it tonight, pray. To-morrow will see us at a better shelter."

A sly-looking, hangdog sort of man sidled in from the back regions and came toward them, holding out a soiled hand. "Good evening, I'm sure," he said in an oily voice. "Asa Wicker, at your service."

Father shook hands with him, but Mother bowed distantly. Sally shrank back against Mother. She had no wish to take the dirty hand.

"What brings you to our humble rooftree? It's been a long day since any wagons have gone by us on the western road."

"I'm taking up some land, Mr. Wicker."

"Land? Surely you jest, sir? Why, beyond this place there's naught but redsticks and swamps and dreadful mountains. Would you be on the way to Niagara, now? I see you have a guide, too. Oh, be warned, turn back. And the wolves is dreadful bad in these parts. Howl around the sheds of a winter's night fit to freeze the blood."

"If it's so dangerous and lonely, I wonder you abide here yourself, sir."

The landlord spread his hands with an upward roll of

his small eyes. "I was fated to minister to the comforts of the traveler from early youth. And my wife—" here he jerked his head over his shoulder in the direction of his spouse, who was moving benches and trestle boards around as if they had been toothpicks—"having the house from her father who built it when Forbes' men made the road, is a rare one for keeping a notable tavern. Why, ask any man along the western road about Ma Wicker. He! He!"

He would have rambled on forever, his shifty eyes roving constantly from one to the other, but suddenly Ma Wicker exploded with another bellow of rage, directed upstairs.

"What are ye about, up there, ye dough-faced pettislumper? The gentry want their beds!"

"If you don't mind," Mother said icily, "we'll go up right now. The girl can finish while we're washing."

She rose to her feet and took Sally's hand. Ma Wicker hesitated then bobbed a sullen curtsey and stormed up the narrow wooden stairs.

A candle gleamed beyond a half-open door. The landlady shoved it open with her fist, revealing a low-ceilinged room containing a huge bedstead which a girl was hastily spreading with what looked like an old sail, so stained and coarse it was. The bare boards of the floor were so soiled that Sally knew it must have been months and maybe years since anyone had scrubbed them. A heavy smell of mice, stale tobacco and damp clung to the place like a fog. Mother lifted her skirts above her ankles as though she were about to cross a muddy street. Sally had never seen her hold her head so high.

"Please to open the shutters," she said.

Ma Wicker was nettled by that tone, that lifting of the skirts. She could act the mistress, too. Folding her arms across her chest, she snapped at the girl, "Poll, ye heerd the lady! Open them shetters!"

"Aye, it's time we got some o' this stink out o' here," the girl muttered, dropping the sheets and turning a gaunt brown face to the light as she crossed the room.

"Give me any of yer sass an' I'll split yer lip fer ye," her mistress snarled. Sally was shocked beyond speech. It was the first time in all her ten years that she had heard grown people talk to each other in so ugly a fashion. Between the smell and the hard, hateful voices and her whole mistrustful feeling about this place, she felt a dreadful queasy feeling inside. She sat down on a rude puncheon stool and burst into tears.

"Would you leave us alone, please?" Mother said in a low voice that seemed to have steel in it. "I can manage very well, I think. Please let us have some hot water at once, and tell my husband I need him."

"Oh, to be sure, ma'am. I jest wanted to see that the room was got right. Poll, fetch the lady some hot water to oncet, and be spry about it!"

Mother didn't quite close the door in Ma Wicker's face, but it was a near thing. Then she dropped on her knees by Sally's side and put her arms around her. "My darling child! What is the matter?"

"Oh, Mother, I don't know. I just feel awful!"

"She's wore out, I vow," the girl named Polly said in a very different voice. She set the candle on a little stand and knelt down on Sally's other side. Through her tears, Sally saw a scrawny girl in a filthy calimanco shortgown, with a patched and greasy apron over it, bare, dirty feet, a bush of wild red hair and two blazing blue eyes peering from under the mop. She was as dirty as Nannie Tatum had been.

"Don't cry, honey. Missus is an old devil to scare you. Feel that cool air comin' in the windy? Polly's goin' to fetch you some nice hot water directly." The girl darted out of the room like an animal and was off downstairs. Sally distinctly heard a scuffle and a slap, followed by loud guffaws.

Somehow, the bedroom was made habitable. Father came up at once, took a look at the horrible bedtick—straw so lumpy and foul a pig wouldn't have wanted it—and stalked off in search of Wicker himself. Fresh straw, a clean canvas sheet that looked somehow like a wagon-cover, and the Redpaths would sleep in their clothes. Sally, her face washed and a drink of strong tea in her stomach, felt better, but not much! After the clean Blue Ball, the spotless Seven Stars, the bustling, thriving Indian Queen, Wicker's was like a bad dream. The thought of sleeping in the same house with that dreadful, cruel woman and that sly, sneaking man was unbearable!

Father heeded Adam's advice. He lay down on the floor near the door on his own blanket, with a rolled up cloak for a pillow, but first he wedged a chair under the wooden bar in such a way that no one could slip anything between the door and the frame and force the bar up without making a great clatter. He put his loaded pistol by his head after warning his wife and Sally not to wander around in the dark and step on the weapon. Supper had been sent up, brought by Adam on a tray. After her arrival with the can of hot water, Polly Casselman had vanished completely.

Adam was not long on talk. He sniffed at the food on the tray. "Dang thet wheel hoss! Sooner than lie in this hog's wallow, I'd risk Shawnees in the woods. This food ain't much, but I reckon it's the best that poor gal can do. Old trollop—savin' your presence, ma'am and missy—downstairs worries at her heels like a dog chivvyin' a deer."

The meal was burnt, grease-soaked and cold. Sally could not touch anything but some cold pone. Mother fared little better. Adam promptly departed for the wagon, envied by all three he left behind in the bedroom. He was sleeping in the choice spot.

Sally's rest was fitful. She said her prayers with a desperate conviction that she needed them very much, holding Mother's hand tightly with one of hers and the cornhusk doll with the other. She was very glad for Father's pistol. This tavern was entirely too much like the dreadful one in the story where the landlord murdered travelers in their sleep and rolled their bodies into a cellar hole to be walled up behind bricks! It seemed like an eternity to the frightened little girl, although she really slept more soundly than her parents, before the sky showed pink through the windows, and Father unfortified the door.

The Redpaths were straightening themselves out as best they could when a timid knock announced Polly Casselman, carrying hot water.

"Missus'll kill me," she rasped in her husky whisper, "but I knowed ye'd be needin' it afore she did."

Father went on down to consult with Adam. Polly hung in the doorway like a shadow, ear cocked for a bellow from her mistress. She watched with hungry eyes Matilda Redpath's careful brushing of Sally's hair.

"My ma uster do that," she said.

Mother looked at the gaunt young face in the daylight. She gave Sally's shining locks a final stroke and hesitated, brush in hand. It was the same way it had been with the Tatums. Sally knew Mother couldn't bear dirt and untidiness. Suddenly she began rummaging in her leather carry-all. She came up with a coarse-bristled brush and a metal comb. They looked more like things you would use on a horse or dog, rather than on a person, but Polly Casselman's red mop was in as bad a state as any horse's mane ever was.

"Come here, girl," Mother said.

Polly came, still listening for that ominous voice from below.

"You look like a smart lass," Mother went on. "Let's see you give yourself a good freshening up. And a little soap and water on that lovely red hair when you have a chance."

"Law, Missus," Polly breathed, "I ain't never got no time to put on meself. An' Missus, she's goin' to take the livin' hide off me—"

"Sit down, girl," Mother said firmly. Sally watched fascinated as she walked majestically to the open door.

"Mrs. Wicker!" she called.

The landlady appeared with suspicious promptness for one who was supposed to be below stairs, supervising breakfast.

"What's wanted?" She looked daggers at Mother. Polly slunk behind the door.

"I find I require the assistance of your serving-maid," Matilda Redpath said loftily. "Will this buy her release from her morning duties?" She laid a shilling-piece in the grimy hand of the startled Ma Wicker.

The woman's flushed face fell into folds of servility, but her sharp eyes hardened. "Oh, to be sure, ma'am. I'll fetch the lazy baggage fer ye." The shilling vanished into her untidy apron pocket.

Mother stopped the bellow Ma Wicker was bringing up from her very toes with a quiet, "Never mind, Mistress. She's here with us already." Again the door closed firmly on a baffled red face.

"Now sit down on this chair, child," Mother said, "and get the worst of the tangles out. Then I'll see what I can do."

Polly Casselman sat down like one in a dream. She took the comb and brush awkwardly. Sally, feeling suddenly relieved and interested—by broad daylight, her terrors of the night seemed foolish indeed—perched on the edge of the bed to watch. Mother filled a basin with the hot water. Polly gasped.

"Now, not a word. *She'll* fetch more when it's needed, never fear!" Mother produced some more of the home-made soap. No matter into what "wilderness she traveled" —as Miss Collingwood had put it—Sally must remember her training and Mother, her soap. Soon they were sudsing away at a great rate, and Polly actually giggled. She never complained once, though the snarls must have hurt terribly. As the crown of soapsuds piled up on her forehead, Sally idly took out the cornhusk doll from its hiding place in her apron pocket. She was not prepared for the effect on Polly. The girl reached out eagerly and almost snatched the doll from Sally.

"An Injun doll! Where did ye git it?" She clutched the toy in shaking hands.

"Why, it's my Shawnee poppet," Sally answered. "A little Indian maid gave it to me." And then she told the story of the bears and the Indian children and the thunderstorm. Polly Casselman cried, the tears streaking with the suds down her thin face, showing how white the skin was under the dirt.

"It's like what the childer played with in the village where I was captivated!"

"You were an Indian captive?" Matilda Redpath showed horrified interest.

"Yes'm. Colonel Bouquet and the soldiers, they brung me back to Carlisle last year, when the fightin' was over."

"But surely—I mean, where is your family? Why are you here in this wretched place?"

Between sobs—it was the first time in months that anyone had spoken a kind word to the girl—Polly told her story. She had been taken by some Shawnee three years ago, and her parents had simply disappeared. Whether they had been killed at a later date, or moved on, believing her dead, nobody could tell her. Like so many prisoners who were taken while young and kindly treated, Polly had become very fond of her Indian family. Because she was naturally a simple girl, she soon fitted into the Indian way of life. Strong as a young horse, the squaw labor seemed easy compared to the slavery she was enduring at Wicker's. Her Indian family had followed along all the way to Carlisle, and Polly had begged to be allowed to go

She had been taken by some Shawnee three years ago, and her parents had simply disappeared.

back to them when her own family failed to come for her. But the Wickers had been in town. The smooth-talking couple had persuaded the authorities that they would give the orphan girl a good home. Before she knew what was happening, she found herself in a wagon with them, heading westward again, bound out for seven years to serve the Wickers like any slave, without wages. They had treated her inhumanly, and gradually she had ceased to care about anything but keeping out of reach of her mistress' hard hand and trying to get a few hours' sleep. She did the work of three women. They half starved her, and her only clothes were the rags on her back. Until it grew warm enough to wash in the icy stream near the tavern, she never had a chance to get clean. As Matilda Redpath and Sally listened in horror, Polly lowered her voice to a whisper.

"An' oh, ma'am—last night, after the gentleman fastened the door shut, the Missus, she said to me, 'Poll, look sharp in the mornin'. The little gal's wearin' a mighty fly lookin' coral necklace. See did she leave it off when she went to bed. An' her ladyship's got stuff hid in her tucker, I'll be bound.' She makes me look that way with all the folks that stays here." Sally's hand flew to her coral beads, while her mother instinctively clutched at the wilted lace at her throat.

"An' I know where yer man's saddlebag is that he lost," Polly went on, wiping water from her face and neck with a black-looking towel. "Missus has it all put away in a little room with other things. She'd kill me if she ever knew I told ye, but that's the way it is."

"Never mind, child. Let's see if we can make you as

pretty as you ought to be. This is your morning, Polly, dear."

The time flew. Father came up and was sent down again in utter amazement. For two females who could hardly wait for dawn to get out of a robber's roost, his wife and daughter were acting as if they had lost their wits completely. He and Adam had managed a sketchy breakfast and fetched boiled eggs and hoecake up to the ladies. Sally insisted that Polly share hers. She watched in delight, as her mother brushed out the coppery locks that now shone like new pennies in deep ripples over a face that could be pretty if it plumped up a little and lost some of the purple shadows under the cornflower-blue eyes.

"How old are you, Polly?" Mother asked.

"I ain't rightly sure, ma'am. I was a-goin' on to be married."

"Married? Who— I mean, how—not to an Indian, surely?"

"Yes'm. Oh, I hardly knew him. His ma and my Injun ma, they fixed it up to be when we was both older, some. He brung a deer to the door of the lodge, and they asked me if I was willin', an' I said I reckoned so. A gal's always better off if she's got a man, an' all his sisters come an' begged me."

"Well! That is past believing!" Mother exclaimed. "And yet, I really think you'd be better off in the Indian village than in this hole." She rummaged in the carry-all and found a clean cotton kerchief and a pair of knitted stockings. Polly had used the rest of her water to wash her feet. Rather than rouse Ma Wicker's suspicions, Matilda Redpath had actually induced Adam to fetch a whole bucket of well-water. The dirty dress would have to wait, but Matilda also took off her own shift, to Polly's dismay.

"Oh, ma'am, you mustn't! I won't let you!"

"Nonsense, I have others in the wagon, if your precious madam hasn't poked her nose in there, too. At least, you can have something next to your skin under that rag."

Polly took off the stockings and tucked them into her bodice, after the shift had been put on. Matilda Redpath and Sally were appalled at the welts and bruises on the girl's body.

"It hurts, yes'm, but I'm used to it," Polly said. "I'm goin' to save these here stockin's until I git me some shoes." She said it in the same tone with which she might have said, "until I get a diamond crown."

When Polly stood forth, clean and decently combed and brushed, she was no fairy princess, but she was a very different girl from the driven, sullen wretch of the night before.

"Tell me truthfully, child," Mother said, "if I gave you some money, she would take it from you, wouldn't she?"

"Yes'm. She'll probably take these stockin's and this shift soon's yer gone."

"The insolent piece! Is there no place you can hide them?"

"Not a place in this world."

Matilda Redpath sighed. She knew the laws about enticing apprentices and bond servants from their lawful masters.

"I wish there was some way I could help you."

"You've helped a lot, ma'am. I kin hold up my head, now. What kin I do to help ye pack up?"

It took a very short time to get their things downstairs and out to the wagon. Sally whispered to Father, and Father went quietly to Adam. The little brown man then wandered aimlessly into the tavern, his rifle cradled carelessly in the crook of his arm. Sally patted Grayling, the big wheel horse, whose lame leg was better as a result of Adam's hot poultices. Just as Polly scrambled down over the wheel after tucking Mother's carry-all away safely and marveling over the interior of the Conestoga, two men came clattering up the trail from the west, whooping and hallooing to the tavern.

At the same moment, Ma Wicker and her husband shot out of the door, one jump ahead of Adam Byles. The little man had his missing saddlebag under his arm, and "Shawnee-Stopper" was leveled at the Wickers in a way no one could misunderstand.

The riders dismounted with further war whoops, Father ran up with a stout hazel stick in his hand, Polly gasped, "She'll know I told where it was!" and Mother and Sally screamed in different keys.

"Call me a robber in my own house, will you!" blustered Asa Wicker.

"I told ye I was keepin' it fer ye, didn't I?" demanded Ma Wicker.

"What's up, Ma, somebody ketch ye with yer hand in their pocket?" guffawed one of the strangers, who seemed to think the whole thing very funny.

"Ye ought niver to leave yer cupboard unlocked, Ma," the other man chortled.

"Just a misunderstanding," said Father, peaceably, rang-ing himself alongside Adam, with the stick held tightly in his hands.

"I would like to pay my score, Mr. Wicker, if I may."

"He'll make ye up a rare fine one, stranger," the new-comers shouted.

Father tucked the hazel stick under his arm, Adam lowered the gun, and the Wickers retired to consult in savage whispers. But the two men, in high good humor, swept off their battered hats to Mother and Sally, and then caught sight of poor Polly.

"Why, take me fer a polecat, look at Poll Casselman! Say, Polly, I got somethin' here ye really ought to see." The first man ambled over to the wagon, fumbling at his belt. Sally, greatly relieved that Adam wasn't going to shoot anyone, nor the Wickers attack Adam, stared at the strange looking string of long, black, sticky-looking things. They looked like coarse tassels of horse-hair with bits of skin attached. He held them up to Sally and Mother as if he were showing off a fox tail or a coonskin.

"I bet you ladies never seed a genuine scalp before," he said with a grin.

Sally's hand, which had been stretched out to take the thing, dropped to her side. Mother gave a little choking gurgle and sat down suddenly.

"Oh, excuse me, ma'am," the man said. "I reckon it do kind of turn yer stomach when ye ain't seed nothin' like it before. But these is Injun scalps, ladies, the real Shawnee! That's why I reckoned Poll here might like to see 'em, too. Might recognize some old friends, huh, gal?" He waved them in her shrinking face.

Father strode over to the man and spun him around.

"Are you out of your senses, man, shoving those filthy things at ladies and children?"

"No offense, friend," the woodsman grunted amiably enough, "just kind of a novel sight." Adam and the gun moved warily to where they could keep the whole outfit covered, if need be.

The two men loafed around to the back of the tavern, leading their horses. Polly Casselman wiped her eyes on the back of her hand.

"Don't ye care, missus," she said to Matilda Redpath. "He didn't mean no harm."

"But to say a thing like that to you!"

"Oh, they all rates me about the Injuns. Call me a 'Blanket-gal' an' all. You folks better pay up an' git. Good-by, an' God bless ye all!"

Polly ran through the tavern door with one last backward wave.

Sally patted her mother's arm. "Mother, what's the matter? Did it make you sick?"

Matilda Redpath shook her head, biting her lips. "This whole dreadful, cruel place! Come, Master Byles, Henry, let's leave this place behind!"

Asa Wicker presented his bill. Father scowled when he read it, but he slammed the coins in the man's outstretched palm.

As the travelers started off, Mother leaned from the wagon and addressed the Wickers. Her tone was soft, but it made them squirm. "I promise you, madam and sir, that if that girl is harmed by you in any way, I'll go to the Governor of the Province himself to see the pair of you hanged and your rat's nest burned down!"

"Matilda!" exclaimed Father, as the Conestoga rolled away. "What ails you? I've never seen you like this before!"

"Father," Sally marveled, "I guess we've got a rare, brave Mother to take care of us!" Father nodded in agreement.

Riding behind the wagon, with occasional backward glances at the silent tavern, Adam Byles fumbled in his restored saddlebag for something which he quietly tossed into a sumac bush. It was a stringy tuft of coarse black hair.

The next few nights found the Redpath party camped out in real gipsy fashion. In spite of rumors and alarms, Adam had seen no Indian sign. Deep peace brooded over the woods. Sally slept soundly in the feather tick with Mother, while Father and Adam lay in blankets under the wagon, taking turns sleeping and watching. Callie would have moaned indeed over her Missy if she could have seen her, skirts tucked up and sleeves rolled back like a country woman, cleaning fish by the campfire. Sally was so delighted over the continuing picnic that she was almost sorry when Father said, "Well, if all goes right, we should be on our own land tomorrow."

"Thank the Lord!" said Mother.

"I hope yer handy with an ax," was all Adam said.

yond the brook were alders and willows, then woods again, a low ridge of trees.

"This is the place," said Father. He pulled the parchment from his shirt and read, "Beginning from the great oak which is at the Fall of Great Stones at the Foot of ye Long hill—" he waved grandly at a huge oak tree, which did indeed thrust itself forth from a tumbled rock formation that looked as if giants had been building blocks there.

"I hope his lordship knows jest how fur his acres an' yourn run," Adam remarked dourly. "Ain't been no surveyors in these parts since the Almighty laid out the mountains."

"Perhaps Master Mason and Master Dixon will come over to us when they finish running their line between Pennsylvania and Maryland," Mother said laughingly.

"At the rate they're goin', an' the way their Injuns is fidgetin' about goin' into Shawnee country, them bein' Senecas mostly, it'll be a year o' Sundays afore they gits where they're goin'."

The Redpaths camped in the meadow. There was a spring of pure water which bubbled out among some ferns and mosses. Sally, warned sternly by all never to venture into the trees alone, spent hours by the spring, watching the dragonflies dart like gossamer-winged blue needles over the cool water. The steady ring of axes and the shattering crash of falling trees made a background to the games she invented with the cornhusk doll. The little dry brown toy stayed in her pocket all the time now.

All went well until there came a solid week of rain. Sally, who had found so many things to amuse her in the dren romped around the trampled, rutted clearing. They were scantily dressed and burned brown by the sun. Close to the cabin door, a fire burned in a heap of green weeds and damp brush, to make a dense smoke.

"It keeps the varmints off a mite," Mrs. Monahan explained. "They bite a body fit to drive you daft, and it's hard on the baby, too." She carried out a squalling new baby, greased all over to discourage the insects. Mother admired him.

"Is it always like this in the spring?" Mother asked. "We never have mosquitoes as bad as this in Philadelphia."

"It ain't only the mosquitoes, ma'am. It's the black flies and the deer flies. They raise welts." Mrs. Monohan pointed to two of the little boys, who were scratching vigorously.

"An' the no-see-ums," said Adam. "That what the Injuns call 'em."

"Is that the thing that feels like a needle sticking you and you can't see anything but a little black speck?" asked Sally.

"That's them. Lasts till July," he said.

With this cheerful information and other adult conversation which Sally missed because she was showing the cornhusk doll to the little Monahan girl, the Redpaths and Adam moved on. The trace grew even narrower and more weed-grown. It struggled over a brooding hill where the men had to cut away newly sprouted trees. Then, almost like a scene from a play, the curtain of trees thinned out to show a small, natural meadow, knee-deep in rich grasses. At the farther side of the meadow ran a swift brook. Be-

CHAPTER

THE CABIN IN THE FOREST

Soon after breakfast the next day, Sally spotted smoke rising through the trees. "What's that? Does anybody else have a house in these woods?" she asked.

"Aye," Adam growled, "there's quite a few has decided to build beyond the Line, it seems. One fine day ye'll all be headin' back with no lands, no furs, and mebbe no scalps. But I warn't hired to give advice."

They came up to a neat cabin, and Sally was dismayed at how small it was. One big chimney, a plank door, a small shuttered window, and logs chinked with dried clay.

"Ours will be bigger than that, won't it, Father?" she asked, while a gaunt woman ran out and almost overwhelmed Mother with questions and chatter.

"It's been six months since I seed a woman," she explained, running a work-stained hand over Sally's bright hair.

Her name was Mary Monahan, and her husband and sons were out cutting timber, she said. The younger chil-

big house in Philadelphia, nearly went wild penned up in the wagon. She soon grew tired of playing cat's-cradle with string, or drawing pictures with a charred stick on chips Father brought her from the clearing. Mother told fairy stories, but to tell the truth, Sally was getting a little too big for such tales. She had a book, stored carefully in the chest, full of moral stories about children who went to sleep in church or teased the cat and were punished by dying miserable deaths. But this she had read a dozen times. She would have been glad now for Mother's novel about Lord Maltravers!

Father and Adam, soaked and miserable, chopped between downpours and huddled around a fire which went out more often than it burned. Mother, wrapped in a shawl, attempted to cook, but had little success. A dreary succession of hoecake, parched corn and salt pork meals got on everyone's nerves. If it hadn't been for the cow, the week would have been the worst one in Sally's life.

Bossy was a brown spotted beast, thin and touchy from her long journey at the wagon tail. She went eagerly to work on the lush grass of the meadow. She had little milk for the family now, as she was due to have a calf quite soon, Father said. Jacob Stoltzfus would have been upset to see Bossy now. He had said when he sold her to the Redpaths the day they left home that she was one of his prime milkers. He was used to cattle with vast, sleek shapes, who ate and chewed and gave rich golden milk in endless streams. It would take this one quite a spell to regain her proper Stoltzfus shape!

It was on the third rainy day that Sally, disturbed by Bossy's unhappy bellowing, peered out from the wagon at the unhappy animal. Father had tied her to a tree where she could circle and forage for herself in the long grass. Somehow, the rope had become tangled in her circlings and rubbed against the tree trunk until it frayed clear through. When Sally saw Bossy, she was heading for the trees as though she knew just where she was going.

Sally called to Father and Adam, but they did not hear her.

"No, Sally," Mother said firmly, "you must not go into the woods alone! She can't go far, I'm sure."

"But a bear might get her! Or a wildcat! Oh, poor Bossy!"

By the time the men returned, driven back to the wagon by another hard shower, Bossy had been gone for a long time. Father and Adam were vexed and worried. From her plaintive mooings, Adam judged she was about ready to have her calf. The helpless little creature would be at the mercy of any varmints who smelled the strange cattle scent. The troubled Redpaths and Adam munched cold pone spread with some of their precious molasses and waited for the rain to let up.

When the two men were finally able to hunt for her, Bossy had vanished completely. She had left a trail plain to see at the start, it was true, where she had crashed through honeysuckle vines and trambled sumac, but soon she had taken to the easier trail of the stream bed and lost herself. Night fell, and the men came back wet and discouraged. If a bear didn't get her, wandering Indians might. Fresh beef was a delightful novelty to them, and the friendliest tribesmen would not hesitate to shoot a cow.

In the night, Sally was sure she heard Bossy bellow, far away on the hill. She also thought she heard the scream of a bobcat. Dawn showed a pale sun through watery clouds. The forest dripped and steamed, and clouds of insects went to work. Adam built two smudge fires and told the women to stay in the smoke as much as they could bear—they sneezed and wept at the smothering vapor—while he and Father returned to their search.

"I want to go, too," Sally pleaded. "I'm so tired of this old wagon I could scream!"

"Yes, do take her," Mother sighed. "I'll be screaming too, if we have to spend another morning together!"

Father would not leave Mother alone in the wagon.

"Do you stay here, then," Adam told him, as he primed his gun. The damp had got into the powder, in spite of all his precautions.

As the two crossed the meadow, Adam plucked a cluster of strong, sweet-smelling weed, handed some to Sally, and shoved the rest into the neck of his shirt.

"Thet's pennyroyal. Keeps off mosquitoes."

They followed the brook for some distance. Adam felt that there was no use in retracing the cow-trampled trail Bossy had made before she took to the stream bed. Sally told him all over again, as she skipped from stone to stone, how she had heard the cow bawl in the night, and the cat's cry soon after. He shook his head. A bobcat, now, would kill the calf, if it was born, and Bossy was too tired to gore it with her horns. The wildcat would not tackle a full-grown cow, unless it was starving in winter, he said. Now a panther—that was another color of hoss! But nobody who ever heard the peculiar, hair-lifting scream of a panther would mix its cry with the mew of the bobcat. Sally absorbed this nugget of woods lore silently. She was interested, but right now she was listening intently. She felt quite sure if only Adam would hush, she would be able to hear Bossy again. She even tried calling the cow, sure that the animal would answer a familiar voice.

"Now where would I go ifn I was a cow an' wanted to hide a new calf? Dratted critter—here I am, the best shot between Fort Cumberland an' the Blue Licks, chasin' strayed cattle like a dern Dutch farmer!"

"I'd pick a brushy little hollow, where nobody would see me," Sally said. "I'd hide it under the trees like a mother deer would a fawn."

"So would I, I reckon. How come you know so much about deer an' fawns, brung up in a city?"

"I used to know a girl at school who lived at Raystown. I began asking her all about animals and things, when first I heard we were coming west."

"Thet were a right smart thing to do," Adam approved. "But there must be dozens o' brushy little hollers all over these hills. I wish the critter would give out with another beller!"

They scanned the tree-covered slopes for signs of rock piles or thickets that might hide a cow. It seemed hopeless to Sally. She sat down on a rock, out of breath. Adam leaned against a tree. The crows had been cawing overhead in swooping circles; far off ahead a bird was telling them, over and over, "Drink-your-tea! Drink-your-tea!" And then, quite suddenly, all the bird voices were stilled. The crows, it is true, flew on after a sudden vicious outburst, but Drink-your-tea hushed as if he had been popped under a box. Adam straightened up slowly, the long rifle ready.

"Something's moving up ahead," he said softly. Sally's scalp prickled. And then, so suddenly that she jumped and gasped, there was a spitting, snarling squall like a big tomcat up the slope, followed by a full-throated moo. There was a thrashing of branches in the lower limbs of a big sycamore tree. Adam went scrambling up the hill, warning Sally to keep out of the way. She felt far safer at Adam's heels than she did sitting on a rock all by herself, so she scrambled up behind him.

And there was Bossy. Bravely trotting in short, nervous half-circles, her horns lowered, she was facing up a vine-tangled bank. On the big first limb of the sycamore crouched a yellow, fluffy bobcat, spitting and yowling his defiance. "Shawnee-Stopper" was at Adam's shoulder, there was a loud report, and the bobcat tumbled heels over head off the branch to fall dead at the roots of the tree.

Bossy mooed piteously. She let Adam take the dangling, frayed-out rope, while Sally stroked her quivering neck. Foam trickled from her jaws and she rolled her eyes wildly. She was glad to see the two familiar humans. And then Sally gave a cry of joy, for, sure enough, bedded down on last year's fallen leaves, with tall ferns curling over it like plumes, was a little creature with a coat like rippled silk and enormous eyes with long, silky lashes. A foolish pink tongue curled from its velvet mouth. Bossy licked it lovingly, prodded it gently until it tottered to its feet and stood, rocking wildly, its nose already seeking its mother.

It was a triumphal procession that returned to the wagon, just before the next shower broke. First came

Sally, leading the cow and almost bursting with pride, because she also carried the long rifle. Adam followed with an expression of acute embarrassment, carrying the calf in his arms, blatting feebly. Mr. and Mrs. Redpath met them with cries of rejoicing.

"Isn't it the loveliest, the sweetest, the grandest calf you ever saw?" Sally demanded, when their story was told. "Oh, Father, may I have it for my very own?"

"Sally, this calf is going to be the beginning of some trading," her father told her. "When the calf is weaned, I looked to trade her to some one at the settlements for flour and needed victuals. If you make a pet of it, 'twill be all the harder to part with it."

"Oh, Father! I don't want it to be traded! They'll kill it! They'll butcher it for meat!" Sally began to cry in real distress.

"Hush, poppet," said Mother, who had been examining the little creature where it lay under the wagon, out of the wet. "They'll not slay this one. As fine a little heifer as ever I saw! She'll be the pride of some farm this time next year."

The rest of the rainy week found Sally under the wagon with the calf most of the time. Bossy needed no tether to keep her close to her child. When the sun finally came out, the first thing the men built was a log shed for the two of them.

The building of the cabin was far simpler than Sally and her mother had thought it would be. It was also much smaller than they had hoped. With so few neighbors to assist in the "raising," the four of them built it practically singlehanded, or to be exact, "family-handed." Callie and Caesar would have been shocked beyond speech at the sight of their dainty mistress splitting shingles, or little Missy mixing clay by the brookside to seal the chinks between the logs. This was at first a kind of gigantic mud-pie game which Sally found amusing, but later it became boring, and finally downright punishing. Her fingers were chapped and sore, despite the warm weather, from the cold brook water and the clinging clay. Only the thought of how the winter wind would howl through any unstopped cracks spurred her on.

Adam was doubtful about building with unseasoned timber, but he feared the approach of winter with an unfinished house more than he feared the warping of the green wood. The cabin had one big room with a fireplace, and a low loft above. There was a trapdoor in the ceiling and a ladder served for a stairway. This would be Adam's sleeping room, kept warm by the stone chimney. It being July now, he slept outside in his blanket. The little loft was hot as the inside of a hayrick.

The fair green meadow had lost the look of untouched beauty that had greeted the Redpaths that first day. Now it was trampled and rutted, ringed with tree stumps and heaps of discarded branches. But it had a busy look, and Sally felt very proud when any of the far flung neighbors came through the forest, axes on shoulders and tools in hand, to help and criticize. McGinley, a shy man with long reddish hair, and his jolly, plump wife, came for several days at a time. Samantha McGinley was as ignorant of book learning as a baby, but kind and merry. She fell in love with Mother, and gave her sound advice on how

Only the thought of how the winter wind would howl through any unstopped cracks spurred her on.

to put in a kitchen garden when the stumps were cleared. A silent German named Dorp also appeared, with some of his sons, and they were a great help.

So it was that before the end of August, the Redpaths were settled in their house in the forest. And now it was time to return the Conestoga and the six big horses to Jacob Stoltzfus at Fort Pitt. Sally almost cried. The wagon was more home to her now than the cabin. She hugged and patted each of the team—Liebchen and Dopple, Brown Girl and Grayling, Hans and Dunder. Adam and Father had engaged the oldest Dorp boy, John, to go with Adam as helper, and his mule and Adam's red mare rounded out the caravan.

The scattered settlers in the vicinity were already beginning to refer to themselves as the people "at the Forks," referring to the place where the stream that passed through the Redpaths' place joined one of the larger streams running to the Ohio River. These settlers had things to trade, and Adam had quite a little load aboard the Conestoga wagon, given to him in trust, to swap for necessities. The small community needed a blacksmith and a miller, and Adam was to try to entice men with these skills to return with him. Until these valuable citizens arrived, flour and ax blades, nails and horseshoes, plowshares and gunbarrels were worth more than gold to the settlers.

Adam and Johann Dorp left at the end of July. They returned halfway through August, with supplies and, wonder of wonders, followed by another train of three wagons, oxen, horses, and a Welsh family named Jones! All this Adam told the interested Redpaths when he arrived at their cabin, for he left the Joneses and their precious cargo at the South Branch. They had freighted two millstones, he said, and were set to build a mill. They had also brought sacks of wheat, which must be planted in the coming fall if the people wanted grain for the mill to grind next year. Such signs of progress were so encouraging that Father threw his hat in the air and shouted, "Huzza! I'd like to see the faces of all those tremblers in Philadelphia now!"

"Thet ain't quite all the news from Fort Pitt," said Adam glumly. "The tribes is still restless. They's been more trouble down in Maryland. The folks on the Conococheage have been sore harried. I hear tell the governor won't let the legislature pass no defense measure. Pontiac's still hard at it. I ain't seed no sign yet, but I can feel trouble in the air. When my scalp crawls like it's been doin' the last ten miles, somethin's goin' to happen. Seems like the tribes would ha' been satisfied after the peace, but too dern many settlers kept comin' over the Proclamation Line, jes' like the hull passel of ye hereabouts. I ain't no Injun-lover, but I kin see how it would make 'em sore."

But in spite of these alarms, peace continued to brood well through August.

Sally recalled the exciting days of getting settled as she sat, the cornhusk doll in her lap, on the stone doorsill of the new house in the forest, basking in the golden light of afternoon. Around her was the clearing, still full of stumps. Yonder, down a ferny path, bubbled the spring where she must soon go to fill the buckets. At the foot of the clearing ran a sparkling stream. Already, Father had placed stepping-stones so that the brook could be crossed without wetting the feet. Opposite the house rose a mighty hill, almost the last of the hills, Adam said. Beyond that hill was Shawnee country. There Adam and Father would set their traplines, come frost, for the mink and beaver, fox and wolf that were to make Father rich. How it could make him richer than he had been in his fine house in Philadelphia, his wife and daughter failed to see. He could have hired Adam Byles to trap for him and stayed comfortably on Broad Street, but for the itch in his blood to see what lay beyond the next hill. He even talked of building a fine brick house with wings and servants' quarters, of fetching bricks in wagons over the long road—Sally had giggled at the expression on Jacob Stoltzfus's bearded face when Father had made that proposal.

Meanwhile, here they were in a mud-chinked cabin of logs. Mother was wearing a calico gown that would have been donated to Callie long since, had they been home. The great bed was set up, and precious fine it looked on the hard earthen floor. A wolfskin was spread beside it to keep bare feet warm. The rushbottom chairs were ranged solemnly against the wall. It would have astonished the nearest settler to see such a display of vanity in a one-room cabin. But even if the room had but one window, and even if the floor was earth, the place looked clean and homelike. The hearth was swept daily with a brush of turkey-wings. Matilda had hung sprigged dimity at the one window. There was no glass to it, but Adam Byles had showed Father how to make an oiled paper pane that let in a dim light and kept the worst of the insects out. Even the little cradle had its place. Sally had wondered about that. "Where would we be getting a baby from?"

And then her mother had whispered that some day perhaps there might be a new baby in that cradle. Ever since, Sally had eyed it suspiciously, wondering if the baby would come in the night when she was asleep.

Sally knew enough to realize that she must help her mother more than ever now. She had spent the morning sewing her stint, something undreamed of when she lived in Philadelphia. She knew some little Quaker girls, very strictly raised, she thought, who had to sew stints every single day. But for a young lady such as Sally's mother hoped her to be, fine embroidery and lace-making were more in order than hemming and darning. Everything was different now! Sally must soon be making her own clothes. Mother was working on some little flannel gowns that looked doll-size to Sally. Were babies really that small?

All these things were running pleasantly through Sally's head as she sat on the doorsill. Father was down in the wood lot with Adam, trimming and hauling. Soon it would be time for another big burning, and then they could put in some winter wheat. Adam was outraged at all this farming. A trapper, a fur trader, an Indian fighter, cutting brush like any Dutch farmer! But Father had said he intended to have something besides salt pork and hoe-cake to eat that winter. There had to be a cabbage patch, too. He must have taken a tremendous amount of advice from Jacob Stoltzfus on the way over the mountains.

The Redpath family were certainly a long way from Philadelphia—and from their nearest neighbors—so it was with a feeling of real alarm that Sally saw a man come floundering across the brook. The last few weeks had been so peaceful that one could imagine the Shawnee moved a thousand miles away and the Senecas sworn to eternal peace (they were supposed to be friends, but you never knew). Yet here came somebody who was frightened, and badly so. He took the meadow at a flopping scramble, as if his feet would hardly hold him up. He leaned against the doorpost as if all the stiffening had gone out of his spine, and he had to open his mouth three times before any sound came out.

"Sh-shawnee!" he gurgled. "Git fer the fort!"

"Here, man! Hold up! Adam, get the jug!" Father and Adam had arrived on the double, and Father was easing the exhausted runner to a seat. Mother came quickly with water before Adam could find the whiskey jug, and between them they got the man's voice into working order when his wind came back.

He told his story, which was brief. Scattered raiding parties, Shawnee, Ottawa, and other Indians, were in the little valley. The Dorps' cabin, the nearest to the Redpaths', was burned. The runner was Si Gurney, from the small settlement at the Forks. He still had five miles to cover before nightfall. Indians almost never attacked at night, Adam said, because they feared that, if they were killed in the dark, their spirits would wander in the shadows and get lost. They could never find their way to the next world and must roam in darkness forever. Dawn was the time to watch for a raid. Si was so tuckered out that Adam volunteered to go on to the McGinleys' cabin that lay some four miles eastward. He departed, armed with a knife only. His precious rifle was just so much extra weight.

After he had disappeared among the trees, Mother and Father looked at each other.

"Water!" they both said together. "Sally, take the pails and get all the water you can carry up here. If we should be besieged, we must have water."

While Sally slipped the wooden yoke that supported the pails over her shoulders and started for the spring, she could hear the dull clunk as the wooden shutters on the window were pulled to. Mother started to drive the cow to the little shed behind the cabin. Father and Si Gurney were loading guns. The same golden light of afternoon lay on the valley, but there was an invisible menace behind the quiet trees now.

Sally felt as if there were eyes boring into her back as she walked the hundred feet between the cabin and the spring. It took an endless time to fill the pails. Dip and pour, dip and pour. After the third trip, Sally's nerve began to fail. How far behind Si Gurney were the Indians? Adam had told Sally to beware of bird calls among the trees that didn't sound just right, but to her ears, tuned to terror, they all sounded wrong. That cardinal, whistling out of sight in a tree, was he a red bird or a redman?

"One more trip, sweeting," Mother said. She stood ready to bar the door. "Go with her, Henry. She's a brave lass, our Sally, but you're all cocked and primed. I'm not afraid to stay. Mr. Gurney is rested now."

"I clean forgot the Spanish pistols in the chest!" Henry Redpath exclaimed. "Run, Sally. I'll watch from the door while I draw the charges. The damp may have got to them."

Sally shouldered her pails once more. Halfway to the

spring she wanted to stop, throw down the pails and run. She whimpered a little because she couldn't help it, but she made herself go on. Suppose that last pail of water was what would keep them going in their besieged cabin until help came? Suppose it was that water that would put out a fire arrow that threatened the roof? She set the pails down by the spring and picked up the dipper. And just then, out from among the trees, running half-crouched, with a tomahawk in his hand, came an Indian!

He pounced on poor, frozen Sally like a wildcat. She shut her eyes after that first awful glimpse, fully expecting to feel her scalp removed with one swoop of that tomahawk. The healthy scream she had uttered in the game at Fort Frederick, when blond Robert Jessup had pretended to lift her streaming hair, wouldn't come this time. She was dumb with terror and hardly knew that the silent warrior had picked her up like a bundle of blankets. He melted into the woods again, leaving a single hideous whoop quivering on the air. Henry Redpath's first shot went wide of its mark. The Spanish pistols had damped, as he had foreseen. He had to use Adam's rifle, and only Adam could have stopped that sinuous figure that vanished into the trees with catlike speed.

She was dumb with terror and hardly knew that the silent warrior had picked her up like a bundle of blankets.

CHAPTER 7

"SHAWNEE!"

THE INDIAN herded Sally along through the woods without mercy, although she was gasping for breath. Thorns tore her skirt and slashed her legs. The perspiration ran out of her hair down her dirty face in long streaks. When she lagged behind, he hurried her on, with grunts and threats. At last, soon after twilight, when she had begun to wish she could lie right down and die, they halted. Her captor made a tiny fire and scorched some of the strips of meat he had made her carry. Sally could hardly choke the food down, but she managed to eat a little. The Indian made no signs of planning to scalp her, which was a relief. He just sat grimly against a tree trunk, smoking his pipe. After a little while, he motioned to Sally to crouch down in the bushes. He covered the fire and sat motionless in the darkness. He seemed to be waiting for something. It could not be an enemy, for he was quite easy in his waiting. After a little while, an owl began to hoot far off in the woods. The Indian stiffened. It hooted again, this time a little closer. He raised his head and hooted in reply.

Sally jumped. It was such a good imitation of an owl's hoot it would have fooled anybody—but an Indian.

Not long after that, something moved in the dark forest. Twigs snapped, branches rustled. Indians wouldn't make all that noise. Sure enough, there was a dark knot of shuffling prisoners, some crying, all complaining, huddling out of the woods between the silent shapes of other savages. The fire was made up again. Sally's Indian greeted the others. They all ate and smoked in greasy fellowship while their prisoners huddled a short distance away and compared notes on their miseries. There were three women, a boy, and two men, all from cabins along the Allegheny River. The Shawnees and Delawares were out again, they said, raiding and burning for the French—no, by gorry, not for the French, that's over, now, just out of pure meanness. The French was through in these parts. Them was Mingos, I seen 'em last week—oh, my pore feet! What ye reckon they're goin' to do wi' us? That's my cow they're gorgin', blast an' dang 'em. Sarves us all proper fer settlin' over the Proclamation Line. Whattaya mean? The land belongs to the people what settles it. Maybe we're worse of'n during the War. At least, we'd a been sold at Detroit or Niagara. Some Frenchies ain't bad at all. Now we uns'll be shipped off who knows where. Slavin' fer some dirty redsticks t'other side the Ohio. And so on and on it went, a despairing chorus of misery. One of the women put her arms around Sally and they cried together.

After some time, the Indians made the men lie down while they lashed their hands and feet together with rawhide thongs. The women and children they let stay near the fire. Then they lay down themselves, except for one savage who stayed on guard. Sally's captor stretched out on his blanket and began a low-voiced conversation with another Indian. This man had what looked like lace covering his features, a different face paint from the others. Where Sally's Indian wore his hair shaved down the sides, with a roach of deer's tail sticking up on top, this man had shaggy tufts hanging over his ears. He wore no clothes but a breech clout. A crude-looking squirrel was tattooed on his chest. He made motions toward Sally and offered various bargains which her Indian rejected. At last, he produced from his pouch a handsome ax with a handle decorated with brasswork. Sally's Indian fingered it admiringly. She began to understand. This other Indian wanted to buy her. He looked far more savage and fierce than the first man, who had a rather kind face under the hideous paint. This other Indian looked like he would be a cruel master.

Sally could not bear to watch any more. She turned her back on them all and said her prayers, like Mother had taught her. After she had finished, she sat with her hands clenched under her apron, trying not to listen to the guttural discussion going on behind her. Her fingers touched the cornhusk doll. It had stayed in her pocket all along. Sadly, she took it out and smoothed its battered features. The little Indian girl had looked so pretty and kind. Sally rocked the doll and crooned to it, "Lully, lully," until it made her think of how Mother used to sing that to her in her trundle bed in the big house on Broad Street. Then the tears came and she couldn't sing any more.

Suddenly, the Indian behind her stood up and took her by the arm. He pulled her to her feet and led her into the light of the dying fire. It was the man with the lace-pattern face paint. He wanted another good look at his purchase. Sally stood numbly with the doll clutched against her chest. She knew now how Callie's mother had felt in far-away Africa when the slave-traders had bought her from the Arab raiders.

And then Sally's Indian cried out in surprise. He took the doll from her hands and held it to the firelight. She could not understand the torrent of words he poured out at her, but she saw the expression of his face change. She had always been told that Indians were stern and cold, but this one was actually smiling at her. He was waving the doll and pointing at it, and then at himself. He kept repeating one word over and over, *neetatmethar* and then, pointing to Sally, "Ingleese—wagon—bears!"

She didn't understand what he was trying to say for a long time. When he pushed the doll back into her hand and patted her on the shoulder, she only knew that something had changed. He turned to the other Indian and began explaining something to him. At first, the strange savage—he was an Ottawa, but of course, Sally didn't know one tribe from another—was angry, but the Shawnee's words gradually calmed him down. He took the ax back and went off to join the other sleepers. Sally finally fell asleep herself, worn-out and unhappy, but somehow feeling that things were better because of the cornhusk doll. Could it be the Shawnee had recognized it?

The next morning, they were all on the trail by sunrise. The Ottawa had succeeded in buying one of the women for the ax, plus a fancy embroidered waistcoat. He had captured the other two himself, and toward noon, he left the rest of the party and slogged off northward with his three weeping prisoners trailing along behind him under their burdens. The farewells were as sad as if the whole party of whites had been lifelong friends. Sally was sorry for the women, bound for a life of backbreaking toil in the woods around the Lakes, but she was glad to see the last of the Ottawa.

It was one of the white men, a wiry fellow in a butternut-dyed shirt, who explained about him.

"Thim Ottawas is born traders," he said, as he plodded along, his captor's loot loaded on his shoulders. "They trade all over upper Canada an' York State an' the Ohio kintry. Some on 'em go clear inter Cherokee territory, with stuff. That feller'll make a good bargain outer thim pore females."

That afternoon Sally's section halted by a west-running stream. The Indians conferred for a while. Then there was another farewell. The other group, the two men and the boy, were taken off by the large party of Indians. Their future might be far worse than Sally's. She had been told how Indians tortured men and burned them. The boy would be more kindly treated, taken as a son by some family, perhaps.

But the men must have learned the watchword of the frontier, "Never show 'em you're afraid," because they went off bravely enough, calling back, "Good-bye, sis, keep yer chin up."

The boy waved once. Then they were gone, among the trees. Sally's Indian grunted at her and led the way downstream. He said something that sounded like *Scioto*. Sally was hot and tired, but she managed to keep up pretty well. She must be getting good and strong, she thought, remembering how she had disliked walking back home in Philadelphia. Now she could cover the long miles without too much discomfort. She shoved the cornhusk doll deeper into her pocket. Why had the sight of that poppet made so much difference to the Indian? She recalled how he kept repeating the English words "wagon" and "bears" when he was talking to her. Suddenly it dawned on her. He was talking about the bears in the berry patch. He must know the little girl who had been up in the tree! If he did, then all might yet be well. Sally had heard that Indians never forget a kindness. If she had saved some child he knew, he would surely protect her. But she still might have to live the rest of her life with the Indians. The thought of endless years without Mother and Father was more than she could bear.

That night Sally's captor gave her the blanket. It was a cooler night, and the mosquitoes were bad near the water. He tied her to a tree by her wrist. She slept better than she thought she would. Whether the Indian slept at all, she could not tell. Whenever she wakened, he was sitting like a carved image by the ashes of the fire. At dawn, he gave her a handful of parched corn from his pouch. He patted the doll and made signs of friendship. She tried to smile. Then they were off again.

The pattern of the days and night blurred, and Sally was never quite sure how long the march went on. They were soaked by some showers of rain, but quickly dried again. The weather held warm and sultry. It might have been the third day or the fourth when the end came.

About an hour after noon, as Sally reckoned, they reached a little stream where the Indian halted. Without paying any more attention to her, he sat down, opened his deerskin pouch and took out a number of lumps of grease and colored clays. He proceeded to paint his face in a most horrible fashion. When he was finished, he beckoned to Sally. "You come." Sally came, turning stiff and cold as his fingers closed on her shoulder. But he did not hurt her. Instead, he proceeded to daub her with the red color until she looked like a bright, new brick. Then he put his things away, grunted to her to pick up her bundles and splashed across the stream. When they came to a little rise of ground, he let out a queer, wild yell that made Sally's spine prickle.

From far away, a wild barking of dogs answered his cry. Then Sally began to hear voices, many voices, raised in excitement. She knew what was happening. They were nearly to her captor's village. Her heart thumped harder. Would she really be safe? Would she see the Indian children again? Would the little Indian girl, if she did live in this unknown place, still want to be her friend?

As Sally came out of the woods into a little meadow with the Indian, she saw two groups of women running toward them. They were all old squaws and puffed and panted as they ran. When Sally's captor saw them, he again broke out in his queer shout. He placed himself firmly before her, calling out angrily to one group of old women. Sally saw that he was troubled. This one group, whose lips were painted bright red, fell back, and a big, smiling woman with a flowered calico blouse hanging down over her deerskin skirt, came panting up. The Indian stepped aside to

The Indian grunted in satisfaction. "All safe, now. Peace Woman has spoken," he said.

let her touch the frightened little girl. The older women exchanged a few words, then turned back the way they had come.

The Indian grunted in satisfaction. "All safe, now. Peace Woman has spoken," he said, and motioned to Sally to follow him.

The next few hours were a strange muddle ever after in Sally's mind. When she sat, washed and painted and dressed in a deerskin apron, on a platform of boughs in the lodge, she did not understand that, in the sight of her Indian captor, she was no longer a white child. She was not even a prisoner now. She was a new daughter in the lodge of Seapessee, the Panther. She sat quite still, her two tight braids of hair hanging down before her. Red ribbons plundered from some trader, were plaited into her hair which the woman, Macqua, had covered with bear's grease to make it darker. The cornhusk doll, the cause of all this attention was clutched tightly in her hands. Sally felt a little like a doll, herself. The whole family—Seapessee, the Panther himself, Macqua, his wife, and best of all, the two well-remembered children, for it really was they—squatted in a half-circle around her. They chattered back and forth like children with a new toy. Still, Sally did not understand that she had been adopted. Her worn-out dress and moccasins still lay in a corner of the lodge. The smoke of the cooking fire hung heavy in the hot air. Bundles of pungent herbs added their odors to the smells of grease and paint and animals and skins that made her nose wrinkle.

The mother pushed a kettle of steaming food toward her with a friendly smile. Sally saw no spoons or ladles except the wooden one used to stir the mess. Dimly through the bewilderment, she seemed to hear Miss Collingwood's stern voice, "Remember, Miss Redpath, into whatever wilderness you journey, you are a Collingwood pupil!" Sally gulped and dipped out a chunk of meat. Bravely, she chewed. It was good. She swallowed it, and the whole family beamed approval. They all dipped into the kettle. The little girl squatted down by Sally. The boy-baby held a dripping marrow bone just out of reach of a frantic dog. Everybody chewed noisily, and when they had had enough, they passed the pot from hand to hand, drinking the rich broth. Sally found herself suddenly so hungry that she didn't mind these dreadful table manners at all.

Soon after eating, Sally fell asleep on the platform curled up on a soft bearskin robe. The firelight wavered and died down. Far off in the woods an owl hooted. Sally remembered to say her prayers. She was so tired that before she could cry for Mother and Father and the clean cozy bed in the cabin, she was fast asleep. In the darkness, the Indian girl moved closer to Sally. At last, she had a sister.

It was not until long afterward, when Sally had learned enough Shawanese to understand, that she realized what had happened at the meadow outside the village. The two groups of old women who had come rushing out to meet the Panther and his captive were the "war women" and the "peace women." They always raced to meet anyone bringing in prisoners. If the "war women" got there first, the prisoner would be burned, and perhaps eaten, if there were any members of the cannibal society lodge in the village. If the "peace women" won the race, the prisoner would be adopted into the tribe. Macqua told Sally about this custom in the same placid way that Mrs. Redpath used to explain grown-up ladies' manners to her daughter. Macqua saw nothing horrible about the Indian practice. It was just the way things had always been.

The Panther's village was large. It was made up of many lodges, most of them built of tree branches and twisted boughs. This framework was covered with bark, grass mats and skins. There was a hole at the top to let out the smoke, which often hung about in a choking cloud and made everybody sneeze. The platforms along the walls were used as seats by day and beds by night.

A few of the lodges were made of logs, like real cabins. The French had shown the Indians how to build such houses when Fort Pitt had been Fort Duquesne, before the Long Knives and the redcoat soldiers had won in the fighting. Of course, due to the trading back and forth when there was peace, all sorts of things belonging to white people had crept into use. For instance, Macqua had a real china tea set from France. It looked so queer, sitting there on a plaited rush mat among the greasy clay pots and buffalo horn ladles. She was so proud of it! Seapessee had an English gun, and a beaver hat with an ostrich plume which he wore on dressy occasions. There was an iron kettle and also a broken clock from some burned-out settler's cabin.

For several weeks, after her arrival at the Panther's village, Sally lived in a kind of dream—not exactly a nightmare, but an unhappy dream where you kept telling yourself that soon you'd wake up and everything would be all right. For a while, she was almost completely cut off by her ignorance of the language. Pretty Leaper, which was the Indian girl's name, Macqua and the others talked to her by signs at first. Seapessee knew a few English words. Sally thought he might know some French words, too; but if he did, they weren't the kind Monsieur had tried to teach her.

She was feeling sorry for herself, a bad thing at any time, but worst of all when one should be at his bravest. Poor Sally, poor, wretched Sally, stolen away from home and family! And it wasn't even her fault. But after a while she began to scold herself. "Stop dripping tears down your new deerskin apron that Macqua was good enough to make you, Sally Redpath! You were being *brave,* fetching water from the spring in the teeth of danger. You were doing your duty like a soldier. Would a soldier crouch under a bush and cry when he was made a prisoner? You're better off than a soldier would be. Nobody is going to tie you up to a tree and pile brush around you and stick splinters into your skin to set afire. Don't think about that part of it. Don't think about it at all. You're part of a family here, a family that means to be kind."

But what about Mother and Father? What about Adam Byles? Were they lying dead and scalped beside the burned-out cabin? She thought of the dazed and beaten Tatums. And they hadn't lost any children. It seemed wicked even to try to be happy here, if Mother and Father were stumbling somewhere through the woods, grieving for a missing child.

Every day now Sally followed Pretty Leaper to the hill for firewood, a daily task for Indian girls. She was also learning to shake out the mats and skins that covered the bed-place in the lodge. She often sat with Macqua in the shade of the elm-bark awning outside the lodge door while the Indian woman chewed skins to soften them before she sewed them into moccasins. There was comfort in Macqua's solid presence. She was very proud of her new child, and her neighbors would gather of an afternoon and sit in a circle around Sally, jabbering away in their birdlike voices. Sally learned later that she was the first white captive in the village for as long as anyone could remember. If there had ever been a greater curiosity, no one remembered it. Even the old men came in great dignity to inspect her, while Seapessee told and retold the story of the bears in the berry patch. Pretty Leaper would take the cornhusk doll from Sally and display it to the other children. But she always tucked it carefully back into the deerskin pouch that swung from Sally's rawhide belt.

After the first shock had worn off, Sally began to think things over carefully. She couldn't be any impossible distance from home, because it had taken her captor and her only three days or so to cover the distance from there, traveling at top speed by day, but resting by night. Sally knew they had walked westward from the cabin by the stream. What she could not know was how far south of west their trail had veered. Seapessee had doubled on his tracks more than once, which had confused her.

Father and Adam Byles must be searching for her she reasoned—if they were not dead! How she wished that she had some way of knowing how the streams and rivers ran in this part of the world.

The sun rose to the left of the lodge every morning (the

lodges all faced south, to catch the winter sun). It went down on the right every night. Somewhere toward the rising sun was home. Lying beside Pretty Leaper in the dark lodge, Sally began to tempt herself with an idea. She decided to take a desperate chance, some day when they all went after wild grapes.

Macqua and the other women had concentrated on a tangle of big, old grapevines that festooned the trees. Twisting and turning like some fabulous snake, they made pavilions of rustling green across a glade where mushrooms grew. One loop hung low enough to the ground to sit on, and the squaws took turns swinging back and forth, screaming with laughter as the vine swing rose and fell. The branches that anchored the grapevine swing rose and fell, too, high overhead. Clouds of pigeons that had been feeding on the grapes winged, clamoring, into the open sky above the woods.

Sally took a turn on the swing along with the rest. Up she soared into the green shade, then back to earth, where a touch of her toes sent her swooping up again. All around was the rich perfume of the ripe fox-grapes. A group of the half-grown boys of the village came leaping along, attracted by the shouts and laughter. They had been practicing with their small bows and arrows. Some had squirrels or rabbits, and even wood mice, dangling at their belts, along with sleek, fat pigeons. When their uncles thought they were good enough shots with the small bows and arrows, they would be given larger weapons. Then they might hope to shoot a raccoon or possum, and finally, the test of a real hunter, a deer.

Sally wondered why it was always the uncles and grandfathers who seemed to do most of the teaching. The aunts and grandmothers took charge of the girls in the same way. Pretty Leaper's aunt, Color-of-the-Moon, was always borrowing her to help about her lodge. Macqua had no nieces to oversee, but Seapessee's sister, Wind Flower, had two boys who were always at the Panther's heels. It was not a bad system; it kept a child from being spoiled by his own parents, and made his parents responsible for the children of some other family. And it certainly kept families together. Some of the men seemed to have several wives. Macqua explained to Sally that such wives were usually sisters who wanted to stay together anyway. The boys the father taught were most often his own sister's children.

It all seemed too complicated for Sally to figure out. She thought of it briefly while she swung. Seapessee's nephews were teasing Pretty Leaper as she dumped grapes into the big basket under the great tulip tree. Everyone was busy, working, laughing, romping. Sally swung on, unnoticed for the time, she thought. She could just see the sun as it peered through a break in the leafy screen. It was far from its noonday position, still in the eastern sky. The trail down which Seapessee had brought her that first day vanished into the woods in that direction.

Sally slipped quietly from the grapevine swing and trotted off across the glade. The trail began between two clumps of sassafras bushes. She knew the fragrant bush with its leaves that were so queer and different. There were three kinds, one oval, one shaped like a little mitten and one with three fingers. Many a cup of sassafras tea had Callie brewed for her Missies from the roots and bark. The Indians had taught the first settlers that trick years long ago. Sally broke off a spicy twig to chew as she went. She wasn't really sure whether this was her escape or not, but she walked quickly down the trail until she could no longer hear the voices of the grape-pickers behind her. It was very quiet in the woods. A cricket chirped among the weeds, a big orange butterfly glided busily from bush to bush, just ahead of her.

"I'll just go a little farther every day," Sally said aloud, "until I get to know the trail clear to where we camped that last night." She was sure that if she went back to the Indian village she would remember as she walked along. She did not realize how impossible her task might be. She plunged ahead recklessly, intent on putting several miles between herself and the village. Maybe she wouldn't go back, after all. The sheer foolishness of the way she was running away never occurred to her—just following a plain trail, instead of dodging and doubling to throw her pursuers off the scent—any Indian child would know better than that. However, after half an hour or so, Sally did some unconscious doubling. She made the big mistake so many people do in the woods. The trail changed in an unexpected way, unlike the one she remembered. It forked at a big tree. Sally was sure she should take the right-hand fork. She hurried along, tripping over roots and catching on briars. Soon the trail ran downhill to a little trickle of water, lost in its late summer bed of pebbles. Sally hopped across, panted uphill and found herself fighting through a tangled mass of honeysuckle and creepers that caught at her legs like snares. Her scrambling progress sent two cottontails bounding away, while jays and mockingbirds scolded at her overhead.

After some time, Sally began to wonder if she was headed in the right direction. Yes, there was the sun ahead, but climbing higher all the time. She plodded on, tired and thirsty, and beginning to wonder what she should do for food. It was too late for blackberries, too early for nuts. She could not snare rabbits with twisted grass, as Pretty Leaper could have done. Grapes were not on hand whenever one needed them. She hadn't planned this at all. For a real escape, she should have her pouch filled with dried corn and meat. The only thing in her pouch was the cornhusk doll, that stared at her with its painted eyes, as if to say, "You can't do it!"

How many windings does this brook have, Sally thought when she plunged down a laurel-choked slope to find the same stoney trickle at the bottom. At last, after what seemed like hours of wandering, she had to admit to herself that she was lost. Even the sun was no help any more. She had forgotten that it moved in a slow half-circle. She had been moving with it. Surely that big tree with the fungus clinging to its ancient bark looked familiar—and the weeds were trampled where someone's feet had crushed them—hers? All her headlong flight had brought her back almost to her starting point. And there—yes, coming toward her up the now visible trail, were Seapessee and Macqua and Pretty Leaper, like dogs on a rabbit track.

They scolded her like Adam and the drovers had done the day she had left the wagons to go berrying. She was really glad to see them, for she had been growing most uneasy. She felt a little ashamed of having upset them, and a little proud, too, of having managed to get so far without being caught.

After that day, the Panther's family kept Sally with them wherever they went. And Macqua saw to it that all the choice tidbits did not go to Seapessee when she cooked. She saved the daintiest bits for Sally. She made her a beautiful pair of fawnskin moccasins, embroidered with quillwork dyed in soft reds and yellows. Seapessee took her fishing in the clear river on the other side of the cornfields. With bone hooks, on lines made of twisted bark fiber, they caught big, whiskery catfish, round fat sunfish and plump, gaping bass. Sally and Pretty Leaper and the little boy dangled bare feet in the cool water and laughed together at the nibbling minnows.

"You are happy now, my sister?" Pretty Leaper asked. "You will not to try to leave us?" Sally had picked up quite a bit of Shawnee by now.

"I won't try," Sally promised her, and really meant it. She knew now that the endless trees that lay between the Scioto and the Ohio were better than iron bars to keep her in the lodge of Seapessee. But something happened at the end of September that upset everything again.

One afternoon, a voice hailed the people of the village from the west side. All the dogs immediately broke into a chorus of yelps and howls. Many braves sprang up and hallooed in return. All the Indians dropped whatever they were doing and flocked to meet the visitors.

To Sally's amazement, a horseman emerged from the trees, riding a big, gray beast that snorted and reared among the frantic dogs. The rider shouted at them, striking right and left with his whip. Two braves, unpainted and dusty, trotted at his stirrups. The man wore a stained blue and white uniform that had once been very fine. It fitted him like a glove. On his feet were long, dragoon boots, the good leather soft under its coating of dust. As he rode up, Sally saw a curling mustache and sparkling eyes beneath the cockaded hat. He wore a sword at his side. A pair of long horse-pistols were holstered on his saddle. All in all, he was a fine, warlike figure of a man. A white man! Sally's heart leaped. She wanted to run to him, cry out her name and beg him to take her to her parents.

As the stranger dismounted, the elders and warriors lined up ceremoniously to receive him. As usual, the women and children stayed modestly in the background. He addressed the elders affably, partly in Shawano, and partly—Sally strained to catch the words, but they were hard to get—in French. His Indian escort interpreted for him when his Shawano ran out.

Then the elders made sonorous speeches in their turn. Finally they turned on their heels and conducted the white man to the lodge of the war chief. Sally knew very little about chiefs, or even if the village had one, but Pretty Leaper made her understand that the tall warrior with the scarred face was the leader of the village on the warpath. He had little to do in peacetime, and if he failed to lead his warriors to victory, he had to retire in favor of another. The old men had the final say about village affairs, but the women, too, had a strong voice in what was decided.

Sally was dreadfully anxious to get to this white stranger.

A white man! Sally's heart leaped. She wanted to run to him . . . and beg him to take her to her parents.

Even if he was a Frenchman, there was peace now between his country and England. She had to see him, she just had to tell him who she was. Maybe he would take her with him, like Lord Maltravers in Mother's novel, rescuing the gipsy. Perhaps next week she would be safe again in Mother's arms—

"Come, Sallee," Macqua's voice was saying. She steered the tense child gently into the lodge.

Pretty Leaper followed.

"We play nice, Sallee?" she begged, catching the white girl's hands.

"I don't want to play now!" Sally cried. She twisted away from Pretty Leaper. "I have to see him. Oh, I *have* to! You can't keep me here!"

Macqua and Pretty Leaper shook their heads in great distress. Sally threw herself down on the bed-place and cried. She cried so loudly and long that Pretty Leaper came as near to crying herself as an Indian child could do without shame. Macqua soothed and petted Sally as she lay miserably for hours until Seapessee returned. His womenfolk jabbered at him eagerly.

He bent over Sally, hot and exhausted from her tears. He touched her shoulder gently. "You are one of us now, Sallee. You are the Panther's child."

Remembering the Ottawa in whose lodge she might have been now, slaving and perhaps ill-treated, if it had not been for Seapessee, Sally wiped her swollen eyes.

"Please, might I see the white soldier just once?" she pleaded.

To her surprise, the Panther agreed cheerfully enough.

"Come," he said to all three of them, "I will show you the white man."

They all trailed after him, across the village to the war chief's lodge. Men, women and children crowded around to stare at the honored visitor. He sat cross-legged between Na-Ma-Tha, the war chief, and the Great Peace Woman. smoking the ceremonial pipe of polished, dark gray stone that had a bowl like a frog with its mouth open. The two escort braves stood behind him, arms folded, looking down their noses at the crowd. They wore only breechclouts and, now that the dust was removed, a faint tattoo pattern showed all over their bodies.

"Oho!" exclaimed Macqua, studying the strange warriors, "What do the Miami people do here, my husband? Are they unhappy that they decided to follow the sun into the west and let the Shawano use their old hunting grounds? Maybe they want to come back again?"

"The Frenchman travels from the white brothers at the forts beyond the Scioto," Seapessee explained. "Our cousins, the Walking People, escort him on his journey to the fort at the meeting of the rivers."

Sally's scalp tingled. She knew well enough what *that* was. That was Fort Pitt, where they had met Adam Byles —Fort Pitt where the Allegheny and the Monongahela Rivers came together—English Fort Pitt that no longer was French Fort Duquesne! Whatever this Frenchman's mission was, from one army to the other, he wasn't an enemy any more. If he was going to Fort Pitt, he would be sure to meet somebody, somewhere, who might know Adam Byles, or remember the Redpaths on their western journey.

Macqua was holding one of Sally's hands, Pretty Leaper

the other, and there were people moving back and forth between her and the honored guest. Short of breaking loose and rushing through the milling crowd to him, Sally didn't know what to do. Her problem was solved in an unexpected way.

Several of the young men, ever eager to show off their ability as dancers, leaped into the open space before the lodge door. People stood aside so the Frenchman could see the performance. Accompanied by several drummers, the dancers broke into a curious stomping shuffle, all the while making the gestures of a warrior sneaking up on an enemy, fighting and finally killing him. It was very good pantomime, especially the final leap of exultation, waving the imaginary bloody scalp. They accompanied themselves in a high-pitched chant that ended with the same mocking yip that Seapessee had given when he captured Sally.

The Frenchman applauded vigorously. He was an enthusiastic young man. He seemed to enjoy the show very much. He was perfectly at home with his red companions, and Sally could see the truth of what people always said. The French got along with the Indian tribes far better than the English did.

Now, as never before, Sally was glad that she had paid some attention to birdlike little Monsieur, back at Miss Collingwood's in that other world so far away. What would that stern lady do in such a situation? Her gaunt shadow stretched across the wooded hills to the clearing near Scioto. It stiffened Sally's wilting courage. It placed Monsieur's carefully taught French nursery rhymes in Sally's troubled head. It made her sing straight to Monsieur's dashing countryman.

Surely the mustachioed French lieutenant had never expected to hear the next item on the program this side of Marseilles, for Sally threw back her head and filled the air with her clear treble:

> *Sur le pont d'Avignon*
> *On y danse, on y danse,*
> *Sur le pont d'Avignon*

The Panther and his family stared in surprise and dismay. The village gawped. And Monsieur, the Lieutenant, put down his peace pipe and emerged from Na-Ma-Tha's lodge to see who was singing French folk songs in a Shawano village.

He came straight to Sally, where she stood trembling, her voice cracking with embarrassment and fright. He saw the paleface child with her straggling light hair, her sprinkling of un-Indian freckles.

"*Eh bien, mademoiselle! Qu'est-ce que c'est que nous avons ici?*" he exclaimed.

"Please, Monsieur," Sally gasped, her meagre French deserting her now, like any child who only knows simple sentences like "*Ou est mon chat?*"

"Please, Monsieur, I'm Sally Redpath, and I want to go home."

"*Mais, ma petite fille,*" the sympathetic officer said, "I cannot make these people release you. But what else can I do for you? Where is your home? Where are your *papa*, your *maman?*"

"She is my child, now," Seapessee said majestically. "I have taken her into my lodge." He took a quarter hour to tell the story of his capture of Sally, with gestures. But he did seem to be trying to justify himself. The officer listened carefully. He pulled his mustache perplexedly. Like all people who wish to be diplomats, he was trying to find the right words. He must be very polite, always, careful of the pride of the quick-tempered chiefs, smooth and pleasant to the touchy traders, forthright and soldierly to the English officers he would meet. And now his whole mission was being threatened by this English child who had no business here. If all the Indian captives had been returned last year, as the treaty had specified, he would have quite a time explaining this one to the satisfaction of the British army. And he was most anxious to keep himself and his superiors in pleasant relations with their former enemies over the mountains. Yet if he conveniently forgot that he had ever seen this Sally Redpath, his conscience would bother him most wretchedly. He was a man of feeling, *parbleu!* What to say? What to do?

"Mademoiselle, I feel in my heart for you. *Quelle pitié!* I must not offend my good friends here, but I will help you if I can."

He patted her head, then kissed her hand as gallantly as if she had been twenty instead of ten.

When he went on his way eastward the next day, he carried in his dispatch case a piece of paper on which a tearful Sally had written in a very wobbly hand,

"To Master Henry Redpath
near Ft. Pitt in Penns'ly'n'a

Honored Parents:

I am alive and Well in ye Chouanan towne (that was the way the French spelled Shawnee; the

French officer had helped her with the word). I pray this finds You in Health please come to Me.

>Y'r loving dotter,
>
>Sarah Caroline Redpath
>Sept'm'b'rAD 1765"

The lieutenant, whose name was Jean Baptiste René d'Yvetot, had produced a quill pen and clean paper from a leather writing case with a handsome crest stamped on it. But the pen was useless without ink, and in the end, Sally had used a burnt stick, praying the letters wouldn't smudge too badly.

Seapessee had made no protest over this message. He did take one of the Miami guides aside and, in a devious way, hint that the letter might somehow disappear from the saddlebags. The Miami, who had a superstitious feeling about all writing, did not actually agree.

Jean Baptiste intended to deliver the letter to the commandant at Fort Pitt without explaining just how it had come into his hands. He was sorry that Sally was not a beautiful young woman. He would have made a real protest to Seapessee, in that case. In the long run, the British would understand that Sally was just a leftover—there must be quite a few—that had not managed to get back to the settlements. Nothing could be blamed on his unit, at any rate. He swept off his hat to Sally in farewell as he urged his horse into a trot.

"*Au revoir, mademoiselle! Courage!*"

Sally watched him grow smaller on the eastward trail without much faith. But at least a white man knew where she was now—and from then on, her heartache faded.

The small tasks and pleasures of the gliding days fell like a drift of leaves over the pain. Time ceased to have any meaning for Sally. The days flowed on in an endless stream. The men went hunting, the women and children tended the gardens of corn and beans and squash. The little ones played in the dust and the old people smoked in the sunshine and told endless stories of the far southern island from which the Shawano people had come. Gradually Sally's grief faded away. She found herself laughing more and more with the other children. She carried bundles of sticks from the woods for the fire, she helped Macqua hoe the melons and corn, she learned to scrape deerskins for moccasins. She found herself beginning to think the Shawano words for things. The summer drew to an end.

One morning there was a sharp chill in the air. For weeks, the sumac and the dogwood had borne scarlet leaves, but now the whole forest blazed forth with color—red and gold and bronzy brown. The ground was carpeted with drifts of leaves. High overhead, Leakaw, the wild goose, honked to his fellows as the great, V-shaped flocks clanged south. Bundles of corn festooned the lodges, piles of pumpkins and squash were heaped in corners against the winter. Sally learned how to dry the roots which Macqua dug from the swamp for their winter meals. Persimmons and pawpaws were ripe, and chestnuts, hickory nuts, beechnuts and all sorts of other nuts came rattling down all over the forest. The children would gather bagsful to carry home to the village, while squirrels and chipmunks scolded at them from all sides.

"Now the bears are fat," said Seapessee, oiling his English gun by the fire one chilly night. "It is Keenee Keesthau, the Long Moon."

The next day, he went off with all the braves on a bear hunt. Macqua was very happy. Plenty of bear's fat and oil were good over the long, cold winter. She would make a bearskin robe for Seapessee, and a necklace of bear-claws for himself. The meat would feed them well for many days.

It was while the Panther and the other braves were gone that Sally met the White Woman.

One balmy afternoon, when Palarweekee, the Summer, was paying a last visit to the forest before fleeing back to the southlands, Sally went for a walk alone. The Indians never watched her now, considering that she was part of the village. Besides, how could a child, and a girl-child at that, find her way back to her people through such a wilderness? Pretty Leaper was helping her aunt, Color-of-the-Moon, to pound corn. The Yelper, as the boy baby was called until he should be given his grown-up name, was romping with his playmates and their dogs. Macqua and some of her friends were gossiping in front of the lodge for all the world like Matilda Redpath and the ladies of her acquaintance.

Sally took a little trail she had often noticed when out with the other girls nut-gathering. It wandered here and there through the woods, along the banks of the stream, and came at last to a huge rock, overgrown with moss and creepers. Sally was admiring the scarlet pattern of the creeper leaves against the green lichens, when she heard the singing. Close at hand, some one was singing, in a high, quavering voice, a song which swept Sally straight back to the streets of Philadelphia.

> I have a sweetheart on the ocean,
>   For seven long years has been to sea,
> And if he stays for seven years longer
>   No other man shall marry me.

The last time Sally had heard that song, an Irish girl with a red Galway petticoat was singing it under the window of the house on Broad Street. Her heart thumping wildly, she came around the rock to see what at first looked like just another squaw, digging under the trees. A brown face under a battered straw hat looked up at her.

The woman stared hard at Sally. "Ye're white," she said finally.

"Yes'm," murmured Sally, who actually had to remind herself to answer in English.

"Come over here and sit by me, child," the root-digger commanded, her voice shaking.

Sally sat down beside her and stared in turn at the woman in the squaw's dress and gray-streaked brown braids. Her eyes were not dark like an Indian's, nor were they yet so blue that they shone out at you to reveal her race. They were ordinary hazel eyes like anyone might have. She had a thin face that was neither old nor young. It was darkened by years of exposure to the weather.

"What's your name, honey?" she asked after a long silence.

"Sally—Sally Caroline Redpath, ma'am," Sally whispered.

"That's a good name. Don't ne'er fergit it. Say it over

to yersel', nights. Remember who ye are an' where ye come from. Some day ye may go home, God willin', an' ye don't want to be like thim poor captivated ones that fergits their names an' families complete. They ain't Injuns nor they ain't white, an' there's no place fer thim but the woods again."

"Did you forget your name?"

"No, child. Me name's Mary Eliza McPhee, an' I was born in Belfast, in the Ould Country. I came over with me family whin I was but a weanlin' babe. We lived in Lancaster wi' the Dutch, an' we lived in Harris's Ferry whin it was the very wilderness of God."

Sally listened as the woman told her story. How she grew up and married a soldier and lived always on the very edge of the forest until he was killed on the Ohio. Being an adventurous sort, Mary Eliza had chosen to live in a cabin near Venango long after she should have sensibly gone back to safe territory. For some reason, the Hurons and Delawares, her nearest red neighbors, had left her alone, but the marauding Shawnee had carried her off to the Scioto villages. She had been married to a chief, Neenotoa by name, a great friend of the French at Fort Detroit. When he died on a visit to this village, Mary Eliza had chosen to remain here. There was no one to go back to over the mountains. She had no possessions but the furs and weapons of her Shawnee husband. The people respected her and let her live in this lodge apart from the village. She knew all the herbs and simples of the forest and their ways of healing, picked up over the years from wise women, red, white and black. Even the village medicine man consulted her when his howlings and dosings failed to help his patients. Sally felt that she had indeed made a friend.

"Tell me all about yersel', now. Ye must kape it fresh in yer mind, fer the day'll come whin ye can go home. Even if—God ferbid—yer mither an' fayther are dead, there's all yer kinfolk a-waitin'."

So Sally told her all about the beautiful house on Broad Street, and Miss Collingwood's, and Lady Georgeanna Caroline Maltravers, and the wagons and Jacob Stoltzfus. She tried to tell about Mother and Father, but she choked up. Mary Eliza McPhee hugged her in silence then.

Presently she began to sing again, the ballad Sally had heard her warbling when she first came up the trail—

> Perhaps your sweetheart he is drowned,
>   Perhaps he's in some battle slain,
> Perhaps he's to some pretty girl married,
>   And he shall ne'er return again.

Sally wiped her eyes and listened. The rambling verses with their happy ending of lovers reunited made her feel better, somehow, and she was able to join in on the final stanza of *The Pretty Fair Maid* with a good will.

She started back to the village as the sun was setting, happy in the knowledge that she had made a powerful friend. Macqua and the Panther were kind to her, but if anything should ever happen, Mary Eliza McPhee would be a tower of strength, she was sure.

CHAPTER

WINTER WITH THE SHAWANO PEOPLE

THE BALMY WEATHER was indeed the last of summer. In the next few days, the wind blew raw and cold from the northwest and the Indian people put on an extra coat of grease, just as the animals put on their thicker fur and layers of fat. Seapessee and the braves returned from the hunt with great shoutings and song. They had killed three fat bears, besides ten deer and wild fowl past counting. The whole village hummed with activity. Cutting and skinning, dressing of hides and melting down of tallow, curing and drying of meat, occupied all the women, and Sally learned how to do her share. Pretty Leaper was skilled in her mother's arts. She helped Sally's unaccustomed fingers to learn their new tasks.

The men were now content to sit around in the pale sunshine, wrapped in blankets, smoking and playing endless gambling games. Sally saw why so many white people believed Indian men were lazy. But it was because the work was divided so sharply between men and women. The men spent days and weeks hunting and fishing, running into dangers from animals and human enemies. The women took over when they came home, preparing the food and curing the skins. Sally learned how to make thread out of a deer's sinews, stripping and cutting them, chewing them to make them soft and pliable. Pretty Leaper and Macqua made needles of sharp slivers of bone. Macqua was the proud possessor of a real steel needle, but this was considered so valuable that it was kept tucked away in a roll of red strouding cloth at the bottom of a bag. It was brought out and admired endlessly, but almost never used.

One night when the first snowflakes were swishing softly against the lodge, Sally and Pretty Leaper were busily engaged in polishing shell discs to make counters for games. The skin curtain of the door was pushed aside. Seapessee rose to welcome an old man, who came in with great dignity. Several neighbors were with him. The children moved back against the sleeping platform to give them room by the fire. Macqua at once pushed the pot toward them, bidding them help themselves to food. She always kept something on the fire for guests, just as Matilda Redpath had always summoned Caesar and Callie to bring tea and cakes when friends dropped in at home. When the visitors had solemnly eaten squirrel and hominy, they wiped their greasy hands on their robes. Sally could not keep up with all the conversation, but when the old man cleared his throat and sat upright, Pretty Leaper nudged her.

"Listen—he will tell stories now. I will explain to you."

So Sally sat quiet as a mouse, trying to understand the words, and Pretty Leaper would whisper the meaning to her when she looked too puzzled.

"Long, long ago," the old man began, "our people were so many and so evil that the Great Spirit, Washa Manitou, destroyed them all in a great flood."

"Why, that's like Noah, in the Bible," thought Sally.

"All, all were drowned, but one old woman. She was carried far away into the sky, where she wept day and night for her grandchildren. Finally Washa Manitou could stand her weeping no longer. He decided to make more people to fill up the earth." Here the old man held his pipe out to Seapessee, who placed a hot coal in the bowl.

"Twelve medicine roots the Manitou gathered, to make a wash for his body. Soon he became pure and white, like the snow of winter. Long, long, he thought, and at last he decided on a way to make more people, better than the first. So he sent out the crawfish upon the face of the waters."

"Noah sent a dove," Sally remembered. She must pay close attention to this story, also, because it was so like the Bible tale. How queer that the Shawano should have one so very much like the one that had been read to her by her mother in Philadelphia—it seemed very long ago and far away now.

But the old man was going on with his story. "The crawfish scooped up in his claws some mud from the bottom of the waters and brought it to Washa Manitou. From this mud the Great Spirit fashioned a new world. He needed something to hold it down at the corners, so he made four large animals who sat at the four corners of the world." No doubt everyone in the lodge had heard this story dozens of times before, but they all listened with breathless attention.

"Next, Washa Manitou made the people and put them in the center of the world. He made the beasts and birds, the fish that swim and the insects that crawl and fly. He made the trees of the forest, and the mountains and prairies. And he taught all his children to follow the great road that leads to Washa Manitou, the Father."

The old man paused and drew long upon his pipe. It was carved in the form of a duck, from a shiny, dark stone, worn smooth as glass from years of service. Looking long and hard around him, he continued.

"As Washa Manitou made each tribe, he brought these people down from the sky and gave them a place on the new earth. He sang four songs as they were descending. Each nation took a song, which is the reason why we sing in a different way from the Cherokee people, or the Seneca, or the Fox. But best of all, Washa Manitou loved the Shawano people, for to them he gave a piece of his own heart."

"No matter if you're red or white or black," thought Sally, when Pretty Leaper had finished explaining the unfamiliar words in a low whisper, "I reckon you think your folks are best of all."

"When the Great Father had given the best gift of all to his children—the corn that gives them food and drink—he taught them how to multiply and tend the little children, that the tribes might grow in the earth."

The aged voice went on and on. Sally's head drooped with sleepiness, and Pretty Leaper nodded drowsily, beside her. . . . The old man had reached to the part of his story where the Shawano began their endless wanderings from the island in the South before Sally was jolted awake by the falling of a log in the fire. She heard the rest of the long tale in a kind of dream, but she would always remember the part about the coming of the white man on the far eastern seacoast. She was sure that the wise old eyes were fixed on her as the grandfather told how the white man's trickery had stolen away the red man's land, piece by piece. Back to the west, over the Blue Mountains, away from the swift-running rivers, the Shawano and the Lenapé and their brothers had been pushed. Soon, the grassy meadows of the western lands would be too small to hold them all. The tide had turned. The white men were rising like the waves of the great waters. The red children of Washa Manitou were breaking like the reeds in the swamp in the dry heat of summer.

"But, my uncle," said a solemn brave with a mighty roach of deer tail standing straight up from his shaven scalp, "did not the Great Fathers Over the Water say that hereafter no white man could cross over the line which they drew on the picture-writing of the land? The line which runs through the heads of all the rivers which run into the great sea?"

"But, my nephew," the old man answered, "did not the Shawano people agree to send home all the white captives, when the great general of the Father Across the Waters came to the fort at the meeting of the rivers?" He waved the duck pipe at Sally where she sat, cross-legged, in her deerskin dress, with the shells she was polishing all around her on the platform. "Yet here in the lodge of Seapessee sits a white child who has been brought since the great general took home the white captives across the mountains."

Seapessee's face never changed as he said, "True. My uncle speaks with a straight tongue. Yet the cabin of this child was many days' march this side of the line that passes through the head of the east-running rivers."

"So two evils have been done instead of one. The lodge of the white child's people has been pitched where no white lodge should be. But the Panther has taken that child into his own lodge and made the white men—and the white soldiers—very angry. Some day they will all come back. And then they will forget the line that was made on the picture of the land. Not one man, but all men will forget. And the Shawano people will be driven like the clouds beyond the forests."

"I saved the child alive, my uncle. She would have been sold as a slave to the Ottawa, to work for them far from her own people, forever. But because she saved my children from the bear, I have made her my own daughter."

The old man rose with great dignity.

"All this I know. Your heart was good in bad, Seapessee. But my spirit is troubled. The day of the Shawano is cloudy and dark. We are far from the island in the South. We shall never go home again."

The old man gathered his blanket about him and went out into the driving snow to his own lodge. Sally watched as the others followed. Macqua and Seapessee sat without moving, staring into the fire. But Pretty Leaper and her brother were fast asleep.

As the winter went on, the village was more and more isolated. No one could remember when the snow had been so deep in this region. Luckily for Seapessee's people, they had laid in food enough to last for some time. Other villages were not so fortunate. Rumors came of hunger in many places. Sally wondered how Mother and Father—if they were alive at all—were faring. Were they in the cabin by the little creek, grieving for her, hungry and cold, perhaps? Or were they safe in some fort or back in the settlement, maybe even home in Philadelphia? Sally wondered about all this as she and Pretty Leaper struggled home through the drifts with the firewood. But Pretty Leaper, bothered by no such problems, was chattering gaily on about a dance of some sort that was to be held in the village.

"When winter comes, we are all home together, so it is the best time for dances," she explained.

"Do you dance around a fire and howl and scream like the braves?"

"Oh, no! The women and girls have their own dances. You will see. When we are older, there are dances with the young men, too. You wait until tonight, Sallee."

That night was still and windless. The stars shone through a slight haze, and the air was almost mild. It felt wonderful to be outdoors, after the bitter cold of the preceding days, and the smoky closeness of the lodges. Sally could get used to almost everything except the way the lodges smelled!

The broad open space in the center of the village was trampled hard and flat. The snow was tightly packed, except where the heat of the fire in the center of the dancing-ground had made a slush. Seated on bearskin robes was a line of drummers, thumping away on drums made of basswood, while some of the people stood behind them, shaking gourds filled with pebbles.

All the families of the village were there, painted gaily and dressed in their best robes. Even the small children were present. Dogs yelped and scuttled and fought on the outskirts of the crowd, babies howled, the young folks laughed and teased each other. Sally wondered, watching them, how these same merry people could burn a cabin and lift a scalp, or torture a screaming prisoner to death. Then she remembered what Seapessee had said about the cruelty of the English in putting an Indian prisoner in jail in a faraway city, where he lingered in a dark, cold cell for years before he died. It was all in how you looked at it. Different tribes had different customs. What was wicked and horrible to one seemed right and natural to another. The well-dressed people who danced quadrilles in the ballrooms of New York and Philadelphia crowded to hangings and bearbaitings the next day.

But now the steady thump of the drum signaled the beginning of a dance. Sally watched with great interest as one of the men shuffled across the dancing-ground and caught hold of the robe of a young woman who stood laughing by her lodge. He turned away again and she followed behind him, stamping and shuffling along. Then an old man twitched the robe of his granddaughter, a girl of sixteen, and away they shuffled, behind the first dancers. And so it went on, until a long snake of dancers was stomping and shuffling along around the village to the beat of the drum. Sometimes a brave would stoop down and enter a lodge, hauling out a protesting woman who had decided to go to sleep early. Everyone would laugh at her heavy eyes, but she had to join the dance, whether or no. Sally was laughing with the rest when she felt her dress jerked. She looked around to see Little Raccoon, a cousin of Pretty Leaper's. He had absolutely no expression on his face, indeed he looked as if he were a thousand miles away. Not for worlds would he have admitted that he was fond of dancing or that he even knew the white girl was around. Sally heard Macqua's delighted laugh. She was happy because her adopted child was accepted by the others. So Sally pulled her robe up around her shoulders and hopped away behind the boy. He never looked back at her. When the dance was finally ended, he darted away among the other boys without a word. But after that, Sally felt completely at home.

"That is called 'The Bringing Dance,' " Pretty Leaper whispered.

Next the women danced in a long line, facing a man who sang a long, weird song. When they had finished the chorus, they all danced around in a circle, while he sang alone. Sally grew very tired of this one, it went on for so long. But she loved the one like "Follow-the-Leader," where they all trotted slowly around like an immense caterpillar, shaking rattles, with each one making exactly the same motions as the person in front.

It was late in the night when the people finally ended the dancing. Sally and Pretty Leaper were sound asleep under the fur robes in their lodge when the last dancer shuffled off home.

Sally had long ago lost track of the days and months. She reckoned time now as the Indians did—by moons and weather. She missed the family celebration of Christmas and tried her best to explain it to Pretty Leaper.... She judged it must be getting on to spring when the days turned warm and lazy at noon, and the snow turned to slush and then mud. The song sparrows that had bravely warbled on fine days all through winter burst into reckless song. Of course, the winter lingered, and there were several more fierce, sudden snowstorms, but they melted quickly the next day.

One raw, drizzly morning, Sally and Pretty Leaper were fetching home their loads of sticks when they met the White Woman. An old buffalo robe covered thin shoulders, a man's battered, three-cornered hat was tied over her braids with a faded red muffler. With her digging stick, she was poking among the wet, dead leaves for the first sprouting herbs. When she saw the two girls, she straightened up and made signs to them to come closer.

Pretty Leaper jerked at Sally's elbow. "Come on," she whispered. "That woman bad medicine."

"Don't be silly," Sally replied. "You know she's a friend. Didn't she make your cousins's little boy well when the medicine man's voice gave out? He couldn't howl any more spells, but Mary Eliza fed him her secret tea and he got better right away."

"I don't like the medicine man either," Pretty Leaper muttered, but she followed Sally down the hill. Their moccasins slipped in the wet earth. Soon it would be barefoot time again.

Mary Eliza McPhee greeted the two girls warmly.

"Ye've wintered well," she observed. She spoke in Shawanese to Pretty Leaper, who answered her with downcast eyes.

"This wan niver needed my herb broth," she remarked to Sally, her eyes twinkling. "Now if ye feel in the need of a spring tonic, honey dear, I've just the thing in me house yonder!"

Sally shook her head. "Thank you, but I hadn't so much as a runny nose the whole winter, ma'am," she answered.

"Sure 'tis the way ye've been livin'. If ye live to be tin years old, ye've a pretty fair chance to live to a hundred, barrin' ye stop an arrow or meet up with a she-bear with cubs," Mary Eliza said.

"I've met one," Sally replied.

"So ye have, so ye have." The woman chuckled. "Well, be on yer way home and God bless ye."

"Herb tea! Ugh!" Pretty Leaper made a sour face as she sloshed through the mud. But she brightened again as she saw her aunt, Color-of-the-Moon, coming toward them.

"What's that she's carrying?" asked Sally.

The woman was lugging a bundle of wooden tubes and a sharp knife. She smiled at the two girls as she came up to them.

"It's to tap the trees for sap!" Pretty Leaper shouted. "This is the best time of the whole year, Sallee!"

The next few weeks were taken up by the maple sugaring, a task which was more fun than work. Every morning, Sally and the other girls would collect the bark buckets from under the basswood spouts. Holes had been drilled in the trunks of the maple trees so that the thin, watery sap trickled out through the spouts which Color-of-the-Moon and the other women had inserted in the holes. The sap was poured from all the bark buckets into big kettles and boiled and boiled over bright, hot fires. Sally wondered how Macqua could tell when the stuff was ready, but after many tries—she did this by pouring a ladleful on the nearest patch of melting snow and then watching the way the sap stiffened in the chilly slush—it would be at the right stage for pouring. It was left to harden in bark trays and boxes. Cakes of the delicious, amber sugar were stacked away to serve as sweetening for another year, while the children gobbled lumps of the sticky sirup splattered in the snow, heedless of the pine needles, bits of bark and dirt that were embedded in the sugar.

By the time that Spring was really on the village, with leaves popping open on the oaks at last and thousands of birds making the forest ring in the dawn, it was corn-planting time again. But Seapessee and Macqua made no preparation for the annual ritual. While the rest of the village were busy burning grass on the fields along the river, they sat quietly in their lodge, talking in low tones. Something was worrying Seapessee. Last year's seed corn was ready for planting, and still Macqua made no move. Pretty Leaper and Sally were kept busy helping the aunts sort out the seeds of pumpkin and squash. The Yelper scrambled in the mud with the puppies and the other small children. But an air of mystery and suspense hung over the lodge.

CHAPTER

THE VOICE OF THE PANTHER

THE MEDICINE MEN came in solemn procession one evening during new moon. They carried bags of great power, Pretty Leaper whispered to the awestruck Sally. When they entered the lodge, Macqua offered them her choicest tidbits. All had been swept and cleaned for their visit and hot coals had been thrown in the corners to drive out evil. The men opened their medicine bags—the skins of woodpeckers and of raccoons. These were filled with dried roots, and strange-colored stones, evil-smelling herbs and claws of animals. The medicine men chanted strange, eerie songs as one of them softly thumped a small drum. Then they smoked and blew long puffs over Seapessee's bent head. As silently as they had come, they withdrew, leaving a silent lodge.

Still Seapessee sat, hour after hour, lost in thought. Sally wondered what was the matter with him, but she did not dare ask.

He was sitting just so one evening at sundown when

Mary Eliza McPhee walked up to the lodge and entered. She greeted all in Shawanese, said, "How d'ye do," to Sally, and stood over Seapessee like some ancient Irish Druidess. "Go to the woods, Seapessee," was all she said.

At last, one morning when the redbud was in bloom, Seapessee got up from his seat by the fire and, without a word to anyone, strode away through the village and into the woods. Sally, gathering sticks as usual on the hillside, saw him go. Along the creek, a bent figure in a faded plaid shawl straightened above a digging stick and watched him go, too. Neither Macqua nor Pretty Leaper seemed worried when Seapessee failed to come home that night.

"What is he going to do?" Sally wondered. "He took no weapons with him, not even a blanket."

Macqua stirred the pot cheerfully, while the Yelper jabbed eagerly at the seething mess with his shell ladle.

"He is waiting for a vision," she said. "He cannot eat or sleep while he is waiting. His body and mind must be all empty before he can see."

Sally said that she thought it curious that Seapessee should remain in the forest for any reason at corn-planting time.

Macqua laughed at that. "Sallee forgets that with us it is the women who plant the fields."

And for the next two days, while a warm sun shone and the maple leaves came out like green popcorn, the women and girls worked in the rich bottom lands along the creek. Macqua carried the stone-bladed hoe and the digging stick. Sally and Pretty Leaper followed with the precious seed corn and the pumpkin seeds in deerskin bags, and the Yelper brought up the rear, bearing a flat basket piled with decaying fish heads. He was accompanied by a cloud of droning, buzzing flies and a smell that could be almost felt! It did not seem to bother him at all, but Sally choked and gasped and kept as far away from him as possible.

Macqua and Pretty Leaper showed Sally how to plant the corn in little hoed-up hills, with a fish head in each hill for fertilizer. Sally would squat between the rows and poke the corn in with her finger, the soil was so rich and loamy. Pretty Leaper followed with the watermelon and pumpkin seeds, planting them around the base of each hill. Then when the cornstalks grew tall, the pumpkin and melon vines could run along the rows between, in the shade.

"So Washa Manitou showed his people in the beginning," Macqua said, expertly inserting a fish head. A disappointed stream of flies zoomed off and settled again on the heads left in the basket.

"A Frenchman from Kaskaskia told me once there was no corn in his country," she went on pityingly.

"There are lots and lots of cornfields back home near Philadelphia," said Sally.

"Who showed the white man how to plant corn?" Macqua demanded.

"I never thought of that," Sally admitted.

The sun beat down on the wide field, dotted with bending figures. Beyond the creek, the woods showed tender green where maple and beech trees had budded, pinkish gold on the oaks, drifts of white where the dogwoods climbed the hill, deep purplish pink on the redbuds. Underfoot, right up to the edge of the cornfield, clumps of violets made a deep purple carpet, varied by the white stars of bloodroot. Along the creek, yellow adder's tongue rose above its spotted leaves. Skunk cabbage simmered in hot green rankness. The mild air quivered with insects, from the small white butterflies that dipped along the rank yellow mustard blooms to the droning flies that hovered over the remaining fish heads.

Sally wondered about Father and Mother. Were they awkwardly trying to put in a crop with their hands so unused to toil? Or had they given up, sure that she was lost forever, and gone back to their safe home in Philadelphia? Don't ever forget who you are, Mary Eliza McPhee had told her. Sarah Caroline Redpath, of Broad Street, Philadelphia, in the colony of Pennsylvania. "Remember, Miss Redpath, into whatever wilderness you stray, you are a Collingwood pupil!" This was all so far away it was becoming almost like a dream. Less than a year—and yet a world away. Sally squatted by her corn hill in the Shawnee village and wiped her moist eyes on her bare, brown arm.

Meanwhile, in the trees beyond the creek, Mary Eliza McPhee filled a basket with pokeweed shoots and turned an idea over in her mind.

That evening, black thunderheads rose silently in the west. They blotted out the setting sun as they mounted. Sally was playing along the edge of the trees with the village girls when the first warning rumble came. She looked up. There had been several small thunderstorms earlier in the year, as if the rain gods were practicing for the season's performance in the sky. Pretty Leaper turned to Sally.

"Remember, Sallee? The big storm in the moon of thunder? You chased the bear people away?"

Sally nodded. She would never hear thunder again as long as she lived without remembering the bears in the berry patch and the rock shelter where she had been given the cornhusk doll. She took her poppet from the deerskin bag which she carried like all the other Shawnee children.

Pretty Leaper patted it, smiling. "It made Sallee my sister," she said softly. Then the first big drops began to fall, and they ran together toward the lodge where Macqua was waiting.

Late in the evening, when the rain had settled into a steady downpour, the skin flap at the lodge door was softly opened. Seapessee entered, the water streaming from his bare shoulders, his face drawn and thin.

The family greeted him warmly. Macqua smiled in greeting, but his two children did not run to hug him the way Sally would have done to her father. There was excitement in their faces, though. What had he seen? Had he dreamed? Had a spirit really visited him?

Seapessee only grunted in response to their eager questions. Wiping his wet body, he squatted by the fire and gulped the greasy stew in great mouthfuls. When he had finished, he wiped his mouth with the back of his hand and belched appreciatively. Without a word to anyone, he pulled a blanket over himself and slept.

At sunrise, Sally waked to see the Panther busily painting his face in much the same way he had done when he had brought her to the village. The children stared as he painted wide vermilion stripes from ears to nose and down his cheekbones to his chin. He put on his leggings embroidered in red-dyed porcupine quills, and tied on a loincloth of blue strouding cloth fringed with red wool. In his scalp lock he fastened an owl feather. A brass gorget, inscribed *"Georgius Secundus, Rex Britanniae,"* hung on his well-greased chest. Thus attired, he rose and stalked from the lodge, followed by his family, at a respectful distance.

By the time Seapessee had reached the council place, knots of people were collecting from every hand. The old men, draped in blankets in spite of the warmth of the rising sun, sat solemnly, pipes at hand, as if they had been waiting for hours. The medicine men and the wise women sat beside the elders. No one spoke until the pipes had been filled, lit and passed from hand to hand. When Seapessee had blown smoke to the Four Directions and returned the pipe to the oldest man, he folded his arms and faced the council.

"Hear me, my fathers," he said. "For many days my heart has been troubled. My fathers know that when Seapessee's people came over the mountains from the old fields by the river that runs to the Great Bay, they left the bones of their ancestors in the fields by that river, under the mountain shaped like a turtle's back. Then the white men came, and my people took up the bones of their ancestors when they went to live by the crooked river that runs between the long mountains where my father's father lived—"

Seapessee was launched on the old, old story of the wanderings from the South that took so long in the telling.

Sally listened in spite of her impatience, because the winter had taught her that the Indians loved to hear these stories the way children do. A certain ritual must be followed, not a word must be changed, or the hearers would protest.

Seapessee went on with the sorrows of the Shawnees for some time. Then he halted dramatically. His voice deepened. "I knew not what to do. If we must follow the sun to the west again, we can never go back to the old fields. Next spring, the white men may forget their promise and come across the line they drew. I, Seapessee, went over that line. Many of my people have done the same. If all men speak with double tongues, no man's scalp is safe.

"I went alone to the forest. I built a lodge. I made myself clean. I offered tobacco to the spirits. I offered tobacco to the ancestors. I prayed to Seapessee, the Panther. I made very great medicine. I made powerful prayers."

All eyes were fixed on the speaker. Along the edge of the woods, the dogs quarreled and yelped, a blue jay screamed from an oak tree, but not a voice was heard in the entire village.

Finally, Seapessee continued. "For three suns I waited. For three nights I waited. There was no answer. And then, as the thunder spoke, Seapessee came! The Panther himself appeared to me!"

There was a murmur of delight and awe from the crowd. The old men sat like so many rocks, but here and there a nose twitched, an eyebrow lifted. The wise women softly clapped their hands to their open mouths. Sally felt a little prickle on her neck. What had the Panther seen—or thought he saw—there in the dark, rainy woods?

"The Panther spoke to me from the trees," he told the breathless listeners. "Creeping about the edge of the clearing, he spoke to me, Seapessee, his child. He came to me as he came in the days of my fasting when I became a man. I took him for my medicine and he gave me his name. He gave me his heart and his cunning in hunting. Now he came again to me to make my heart new.

"I, Seapessee, go over the mountains to the valley by the crooked river between the long mountains in the South. I will dig up the bones of my father's father. I will bring them back that they may be kept with my people until we follow the sun again."

Macqua's face never changed. Its look of simple wonder was reflected in Pretty Leaper's expression. But Sally shivered as the Panther went on.

"I will take back this child I took from the white man. I will give back my daughter who saved my children from the bear people. Then my heart will be clean before Washa Manitou. I have spoken."

Sally sat stunned while the village boiled around her. Pretty Leaper was crying. People who said Indians never showed how they felt were very, very wrong, Sally thought. Macqua was hugging her awkwardly. Women patted her face and chattered at her. The elders and the wise women shook their heads ominously together. If the Panther had spoken in this fashion to Seapessee, other men would be seeing visions, too. A vast uneasiness rippled through the village. And Seapessee, looking at Sally where she sat in the midst of the chattering women, turned and stalked back to the lodge and crouched with his face bowed to the ground.

CHAPTER 10

AGAIN THE HOUSE IN THE FOREST

The family traveled in single file through the woods, with Seapessee trotting ahead. Macqua followed, Sally and Pretty Leaper came behind her, and the Yelper brought up the rear. Sally remembered how the Tatums had straggled down the Sideling Hill on their way back to Tidewater, with their pitiful belongings on their backs. But they had gone with sorrow dogging their heels. Sally Redpath was going home! She knew she ought to feel sorry for Seapessee, but he had been the cause of the whole thing. He had stolen her, she kept telling herself, to sell to the Ottawas, and only the cornhusk doll had saved her. And just think how he had made her own father and mother grieve! They probably thought she was dead—or a pitiful slave! And yet, the more she looked at that lean brown back loping down the eastward trail ahead of her, the sorrier Sally felt for it.

As for Pretty Leaper, she seldom let go of Sally's hand.

She said little, but her cheeks were streaked with tears. Macqua had accepted the edict of the Panther without question, but she had kept Sally close to her all during two days before they had set out on their journey. She dressed the white girl in a beautiful robe of fawnskin, fringed and worked with quills, and replaced her worn moccasins with new ones made in the winter evenings. For all her wild delight at going home, Sally dreaded the moment when she must say good-by to her Shawano family. She had the strangest feeling that she was being pulled into two pieces.

As she trotted down the trail, one piece was being pulled away and left behind. The village was pulling from back there. That pull grew feebler and feebler, until on the third morning of their journey, when Sally thought she recognized a little stream they crossed as one where she had camped with Seapessee in the first days of her captivity, it stopped pulling entirely. A new, exciting force was pulling her now, from the east this time, and making Sally's heart beat faster as they marched.

"You won't forget me, Sallee?" Pretty Leaper was pleading.

"Never, never," Sally assured her. She wished she had something to give her Shawano sister. Lady Georgeanna Maltravers had journeyed back to James River. Sally had nothing, not even a shred of the clothing that she had worn when she was captured. The only locks of hair that Indians cherished were scalp locks, she thought, with a rueful smile. If only she had a necklace to give Pretty Leaper, or a ring, like the maidens in ballads. Even the Pretty Fair Maid had given her lover a token to remember her by. And that made her think of Mary Eliza McPhee! She owed that wise old woman a debt that could never be paid in this world. It was Mary Eliza who was sending her home.

The morning after Seapessee had startled the village with the account of his vision, Sally had gone to the woods to look for willow shoots to make a basket to carry fish. Pretty Leaper had remained in the lodge, helping Macqua pack their few supplies for the journey they were going to take. And by the creek, still digging for pokeweed shoots, Sally saw Mary Eliza McPhee, in her battered felt hat and plaid shawl.

"Good morning, Mrs. McPhee," she said timidly.

" 'Tis a good morning, darlin'," the old woman replied, leaning on her digging stick. "Me heart's that filled with joy for ye. I'm hearin' good news about ye. Ye're goin' home!"

"Yes, isn't it wonderful?" And Sally burst into tears.

"Tell me the truth, child. Are ye truly happy to be leavin' the Shawano?"

"Yes, oh yes!" But somehow, Sally didn't feel altogether right.

"Good! Thin I caught ye in time."

"What do you mean, ma'am?"

"Ye see what happened to me— I stayed so long I turnt into an Injun meself. I married an Injun. I lived with 'em till Mary Eliza McPhee was almost forgot. But ye've been here less than a year, an' ye seemed happy enough, this winter, from what I could see. 'Tis whin ye're young that ye fergit easy. But 'twas not what I wanted fer ye, Sally Redpath, wid yer fayther an' mither pinin' fer ye over the hills. Do ye be comin' to the house a minute, honey dear."

Sally wiped her eyes and followed the queer old woman through the trees to the smoky little lodge where she lived among her bundles of herbs and dried roots. She had a real wooden bedstead with a cornhusk tick and a buffalo hide for a blanket. She had a copper tea kettle and china cups, a spinning wheel that hadn't been used for thirty years, and a rifle like Adam Byles's. She made Sally sit on the bed while she hung up her shawl and laid the pokeweed down by the fire.

"Now tell me, child, do ye believe Seapessee, bad cess to th' ould sinner, saw the Panther t'other night?"

"I don't know," confessed Sally. "He really thought he did."

"He did, Sally Redpath. He saw the Panther, all right."

"How do you know? Do you believe he saw it?"

"You can see it, too."

"What do you mean? Pray, ma'am, I'm so mixed up in my mind, I quite believe I could see most anything, but I don't believe in spirits—"

"Set ye there. This sperrit ye kin belave in."

As she spoke, the old woman took a bundle from the corner and slowly unfolded it. Rocking back and forth in chuckling delight, she flung something tawny and sleek over her shoulders. There was a rattle of claws. Mary Eliza McPhee shrugged and ducked and the grinning mask of a big cat fell forward over her wrinkled face.

"Now do ye see? Sure, 'tis the Panther himself I am now!"

Sally shrieked with delight and understanding, "You were the panther! Oh, Mrs. McPhee!"

"That I was, that I was. Sure, 'twas so dark, wi' the rain an' all, 'tis a wonder I looked like aught but a bogle to himself, there. But what with his empty belly and his head full o' black magic, this ould panther skin turned the trick. Oh, 'twas a plenty o' advice I give him. I hadn't two redsticks for husbands, on top of McPhee, rest his sowl, without havin' picked up a few tricks o' the tongue. I fair greased him. An' win, wi' a final screech that would ha' done credit to the divvil himself, I tuk off through the rain, Seapessee was flat on his face in the mud."

Sally hugged Mary Eliza, panther skin and all.

The old Irishwoman had stood apart from the others when the family of Seapessee set out on their backward journey. Her only farewell had been a casual wave of the hand. Sally had waved in reply. When the travelers crossed the grassy meadow where the Peace Women had rushed out to greet them, ten months ago, Sally looked back. Mary Eliza McPhee was gone.

Now, this third morning of their journey from the village, Sally could see something familiar about the country through which they were traveling. This proved that she was an observant child, considering how frightened she had been during the days and nights when she had been hurried through it by Seapessee. Also, perhaps her Indian year had sharpened her young senses. She saw the swelling crest of a familiar hill grow dark ahead; caught a glimpse of a swift-running stream, downhill through tree trunks. Her heart began to hammer. She turned to Pretty Leaper.

"I think I know where I am!" she exclaimed breathlessly.

"Sallee's lodge is near?" Pretty Leaper asked. She stopped in her tracks.

Seapessee and Macqua continued downhill ahead of the two girls. The Yelper came up to them and stood.

"Oh, how Adam Byles will stare!" Sally cried. "I've brought a real, live Shawnee family home with me, and they're my friends!"

Sally giggled almost hysterically. Seizing Pretty Leaper by the hand, she raced to catch up with Macqua and Seapessee.

"We're nearly there!" she gasped as she caught up to them.

Seapessee kept going as though he had not heard her. Macqua put a hand on her shoulder.

"Sallee's people will not want to see us," she said quietly. "They would greet us with bullets."

"But you're my friends! You're my other family!"

"But you're my friends! You're my other family!"

"You are our daughter. We painted your face and greased your hair and dressed you in the clothes of a Shawano girl. You are our daughter, but Macqua is not your mother. The white woman in that lodge is your mother. Some day you will forget Macqua. If the Panther had not spoken to Seapessee, you would have forgotten your white mother, too, before many moons."

There was something sad and dreadful in Macqua's voice that made Sally's heart ache. Seapessee turned and came back to them.

He put his sinewy hands on Sally's shoulders and looked down at her with his unwinking stare.

"Our trails fork, here, Sallee," he said. "The Panther will always remember it was Sallee who sent his children safe back to him. But Shawano people will always be the friends of the people of Sallee."

"And my people will always be your friends, Seapessee! Please come home with me. I want my father and mother to meet you—"

"Sallee's father would lift the scalp of Seapessee," the Panther said, his features almost breaking into a smile.

Pretty Leaper hugged Sally. "Some day we will come back and then we be sisters again," she promised.

She patted the cornhusk doll in her hiding place in Sally's pouch. The Yelper said nothing, but his round face was solemn and worried.

"Go down the hill, Sallee," Seapessee said. "You are safe. We will not go until you can see the smoke of your lodge. If your people have gone, we will wait for you."

Sally knew Indians never really said good-bye. She turned and ran blindly down the rest of the hill. The little stream with its steppingstones, the ploughed field with its straggling rows—everything was almost as she had seen it. And there—yes, there, in the midst of the stumps, was the cabin! It stood with open door, a thin finger of smoke rising from the stone chimney. The cow, the same spotted bossy with the crooked horn, browsed in the pasture.

Sally turned to wave once more—but the woods had swallowed Seapessee and his family into their green secrecy as if they had never been. From now on, her face was turned toward home. There was no going back.

She crossed the steppingstones. Now she was stumbling across the freshly ploughed furrows, noticing that there was a patch of well-sprouted wheat down by the woods. Where would her parents be? Would Mother be in the cabin? Would Father be in the shed? Her heart was pounding now, a drum throbbing in her chest. She hardly dared enter the open door. It took a minute to adjust her eyes to the darkness of the little room. Everything looked the same. The big bed, the grandfather clock, the cradle—But wait! Something was different about that cradle—

Sally knelt down beside it. The cradle was not empty. There was a sheet, tucked carefully around the little quilted pad, and a tiny pillow. And from the wooden hood of the cradle there dangled a toy that Sally remembered dimly—a silver ring with little coral beads that rattled when it swung. On the hearth, the copper kettle began to purr as a tongue of flame flickered above a broken stick.

Sally sprang to her feet and ran outdoors, heading for the field behind the house. It had been scarcely more

178 • THE CORNHUSK DOLL

than a clearing when she left, now the trees had retreated almost to the spring. And there—there, coming toward her, was a figure in a long blue gown, a figure with a little bundle in its arms that squirmed and cooed. There was a man's tall figure behind it, with an ax over its shoulder.

Sally saw their faces now, with a light upon them like morning breaking. She started to run. With outspread arms, the cornhusk doll bouncing in the deerskin pouch against her Shawnee gown, Sally Redpath went to meet them, crying, "Mother! Father! I'm home!"

CHAPTER

HOME!

For a stunned moment the three figures fused and were still. The woods around the clearing revolved dizzily before Sally as Father's rough shirt was crushed against her cheek. Mother's arms received her like a haven of refuge. It seemed almost too much to bear, but a sudden mighty squall from the bundle that Mother had put down hastily in the grass brought shaky laughter to their lips.

Mother released Sally, who still clung to Father, and picked up the protesting bundle. "There, there, boy-child," she soothed, between tears and laughter, "it's your sister come home to you at last!"

Mother put the baby into Sally's arms. Two huge blue eyes looked up at her from a face as round and rosy as a ripe pippin. A toothless mouth reached for her finger. The baby kicked mightily at its wrappings.

"Oh, the sweet, the love—oh, Mother, isn't he darling?"

"Glad you like him, too," Father said, blowing his nose mightily.

"What's his name?"

"Jonathan," Mother told her. "Come into the house. I need to sit down, my legs are that weak."

And so the four crowded into the cabin that looked like a palace to Sally. She was enthroned on one of the rush-bottomed chairs, holding the baby, who had fastened a petal-soft hand onto her finger with a stout grip. While Mother began stripping off the travel-stained moccasins and heating water, Sally quickly told about her capture and her adoption by the Panther's family.

"How fair these are," Mother said grudgingly, running her finger over the quillwork. "And almost new. Oh, my sweet, was *she* good to you?" And putting her head down in Sally's lap, against the baby, she burst into a flood of healing tears.

"Macqua made them for me for a farewell gift." A big tear ran down Sally's nose and dropped into the baby's mouth. He made a horrible face and started to howl. Father, awkwardly patting first one and then the other, finally went to the door. He cleared his throat violently and began to halloo lustily for Adam Byles.

Five minutes later, Adam arrived on the run.

"Do ye have to beller me out of a week's growth," he panted, and then the words went clean out of him. The little brown man leaned against the door jamb and gulped.

"Adam! Adam Byles!" Sally thrust the baby at Mother, sprang to her feet and threw her arms around him in a wild bear hug.

"So they brung ye back," he said at last, completely outdone. "God help thet snake of a Shawnee if I ever git my sights on him!"

"Oh, Adam, Seapessee is my friend! He was kind to me. He saved me—"

And so Sally had to tell more of her story to an audience who drank in every word. When Sally reached the part about Lieutenant d'Yvetot and the letter, two of her hearers jumped up at the same moment, and reached for the key of the ironbound chest by the hearth.

Adam got it first and unlocked the chest, but it was Father who fumbled among papers for a carefully wrapped parcel. Inside was a leather cover, like that of a small book, which it actually was—an old ledger—with the pages ripped out. Father handed this to Sally. She opened it in growing excitement. Yes, there was her precious letter, much creased and stained. The charcoal writing was smudged, but still readable.

"I didn't think it would ever truly get to you," Sally gasped. "Did Monsieur the Lieutenant come here himself?"

" 'Twas me that got it," Adam Byles declared, his eyes flashing.

"Middle of October, I think it was," Father broke in. "Things were so quiet I judged it safe for Adam to go—"

"I was at Fort Pitt, tradin', the day o' the first hard frost—"

"Yes, never an Indian had we seen since the day Sally was taken," Mother put in. Adam glared at them.

"If ye're all through—"

They subsided meekly.

"As I was sayin', I was at Pitt. An' who should come

shoulderin' through the crowd, but this barelegged, redshanks of a MacGregor that's a sergeant in the 42nd. He traded me a whoppin' big stone brooch oncet fer a prime beaver pelt, jist afore the siege o' the fort. Said it was his great-grandpappy's in the old kintry, had kind of a history—"

"Never mind his great-grandfather's brooch, Adam," Mother said, "Tell about meeting the Colonel—"

"I'm comin' to it, ma'am. How's Miss Sally to know who Sergeant MacGregor is, if'n I don't tell her? Well, here comes Mac, straight up to me. An' me thinkin' he's got more o' the family jewels to swap fer pelts, I says to him, I says, 'Howdy, MacGregor, that fur pouch o' yours looks kind o' moth-eaten, what have ye got to trade fer a fine raccoon skin?' An' he says, 'Adam Byles, is it?' 'It is,' I says, 'as if ye didn't know it!' An' he says, 'Ken ye aught of a family named Redpath that dwells in yer parts?'

" 'Aye, to be sure,' says I, 'I guided them into the Ohio lands this summer past.' "

" 'Mon, 'tis beyond belief,' says he. 'Come wi' me to the Colonel.' An' away we go, double-quick, to the Colonel's office."

"Go on, Adam," begged Sally, as the little man paused for a drink of water. "I never heard you say so much at once before!"

" 'Halt, who goes there?' says the sintry before the Colonel's door.

" 'Sergeant MacGregor, wi' Adam Byles, to see the Colonel,' says Mac.

" 'Pass, Sergeant MacGregor an' Adam Byles,' says the sintry, openin' the door. An' there sits the Colonel hisself, an' a Major, an' half the young officers, an' right in the midst of the bunch, a Frenchy officer as comfortable as ye please—"

"Monsieur d'Yvetot!" cried Sally, her eyes shining. "How could I have ever doubted he'd get there?"

"Mounseer Divvytoe, or whatever ye choose to call 'im. All smiles he is, an' I've had that white uniform in my rifle sights many's the time in the old days! Well, Mac he saluted, an' me, bein' no soldier, thank God, I stand there takin' it all in. A rare fine show, it is, I thinks.

"'Sergeant MacGregor, reportin' as requested, sir-r-r,' says Mac.

"'Is this the man?' says the Colonel.

"'Aye, sir-r-r, this is Adam Byles, an' he kens the Redpath family.'

"'Byles,' says the Colonel, 'you are acquainted with a family named Redpath, living in the Ohio country?'

"'That's right,' I says. 'I guided 'em out from Fort Cumberland. We passed through here early this summer.'

"'So did a lot of families. And where did you leave these people, Byles?' he says. Well, I reckon that was when my scalp ha'rs started to tickle. If'n I told him straight out whar we was fixed, we all might be in a peck o' trouble. An' if'n I didn't, we might be in worse. Thar on the table was a big map, all unrolled, an' runnin' smack acrost it from top to bottom was that blasted red Proclamation Line. So I looked the Colonel between the eyes an' says, 'I left 'em on Sore Trouble Run.' Which was the truth, fer ever since we'd lost ye, Sally, that was the name I called this place by, an' it's on no map that was ever drawn.

"Well, the officers, they paw over the map, an' not

findin' it, they ain't too put out, fer thar's no two maps alike in these parts, an' maps made in London from somebody's scribble by a campfire ain't likely to have every run in the Western Lands on 'em.

" 'Has this family lost a child to the Shawnee?' says the Colonel. It was like somebody kicked me in the pit o' the stummick. Fer a minute I couldn't say a word.

" 'Aye, that they have,' I finally manages to say. 'An' savin' yer presence, ye were supposed to have put a stop to all that.'

" 'Circumstances, circumstances, my man! Mind your tongue!' says he, red as a turkeycock. 'This gentleman is Lieutenant (he calls it Leftenant, like all thim Britishers do) Divvytoe of the French garrison at Vincennes,' says he. Blessed if the Mounseer didn't git up an' favor me with a bow that nigh swept the map off the table."

"Oh, Adam, he was the politest man I've ever seen," cried Sally.

" 'Pleased to meet ye,' says I.

"Then the Colonel picks up a piece o' paper an' hands it to me. 'Read it, Byles,' he says. ' 'Tis a heart-rendin' document.'

" 'It may be all that,' says I, 'but I'd never know it. Ye'll have to read it to me.' Who did he think I was, readin' a letter like I'd had any larnin'?"

"Oh, Adam, I'm going to teach you to read," said Sally.

"Thank ye kindly, no. Long's I kin read Injun sign an' animal sign, I'll pass up the rest. So he puts on a pair o' them silver-edged things over his long nose, an' commences fer to read. Whin I heered what it said, I jest let out a whoop that would ha' made a redstick look pale!"

"I wish I could see Monsieur d'Yvetot himself, some day, to tender our proper thanks," said Mother, wiping her eyes.

"And then what happened?"

"Then they asked me would I promise faithfully to deliver the letter, an' Mounseer the Frenchy bowed some more, an' they all nodded at me, an' the Colonel said, 'That's all, MacGregor, dismissed!'"

"But that wasn't all, surely?" Sally was disappointed.

"Well, after I had the letter all safe in my shirt, between two pieces o' bark, Mac gits this old book thing from the factor at the tradin' post to keep it from gittin' wuss tore. People was all interested, an' talkin'—you niver heard sich a pother. Women was all fer gittin' up a petition to turn out the regiment an' make a foray to bring ye back."

"Mercy! If they had, Seapessee might have gotten hurt, or even killed. I reckon I'm just as glad they didn't," Sally said.

"They had other fish to fry, it seems. But ye warn't fergotten. I'll be bound thar's men on the Scioto this minute that're keepin' an eye open fer a gal child named Sally Redpath."

"And the only thing that kept your father and Adam from going straight off to fetch you was my condition," Mother explained.

"I couldn't leave your mother alone with the nearest cabin four miles away," Father said. "I'll admit that until Adam brought back your letter, I was nigh mad with worry and not knowing what to do. Once we thought of going on foot to the fort and trying to hire a wagon to carry us back to the settlements. I dreaded the thought of your mother wintering here, and yet, not knowing what was our Sally's fate, I scarcely dared to move."

"Heaven must have sent Monsieur d'Yvetot through the Shawnee village," Mother sighed.

"And then," Father went on, "there was such a winter as I had never dreamed of—we could not have stirred from here if we would. Adam made snowshoes, like the tribes in the north fare forth on."

" 'Twere a good winter fer trappin', though," Adam observed. "I'll never larn ye to bait without smellin' up the trap, mayhap, but ye'll make a fair profit off'n yer peltries afore I'm done with ye."

"We would have perished but for Adam," Mother said.

"Babes in the woods," Father admitted. "Over and over I ask myself, was I mad to turn my back on a comfortable living to come like any poor backwoodsman to this wild place for the sake of this wild venture?"

"No," said Adam drily, "Heaven sent me along o' Mounseer Divvytoe. With me along, ye can soon be managin' yer own snug factory. Me an' t'other men hereabouts to do yer trappin', you to buy the furs on shares—aye, we'll all make a good thing out of it, unless they chase us back over the Line."

"I confess that troubles me now," Father said.

"But Sally hasn't told us the rest of her story," cried Mother. "The child is not home one hour before you're talking furs again!"

"Forgive me, Daughter." Father came and sat at Sally's feet as she went on with her tale. They all listened with quickened breath as she told about Mary Eliza McPhee and the Panther's medicine dream. And when she was unable to speak, for a moment, as she told of her final parting with Seapessee and Macqua and the two children, Mother murmured, "God bless her! And God be with Mary Eliza McPhee to the end of her days. I could almost wish that red demon a safe journey back with his grandfather's old bones, for the sake of his wife and children. Oh, Henry," she went on, "there must be something we can do for Mrs. McPhee! We owe her a debt we can never pay!"

"Could we send to Philadelphia for a beautiful present?" asked Sally eagerly. "A fine India shawl? She has only that old, raggedy, plaid thing."

"We shall see, child. If money can buy it, and I can send word to Uncle Jasper, she shall have whatever you say."

"Uncle Jasper knows about your being stolen, but not about Jonathan," Mother said. "What a letter we shall have to write him! And Grandmother Murray, too. She must be sore distressed at not hearing."

So peace returned with Sally to the cabin on "Sore Trouble Run." Adam declared he would change the name, and Mother suggested, "Happy Return." Father said they had never really given the grant of land a name, and "Happy Return" would be an excellent choice. But Sore Trouble Run should remind them in days to come of the hardships that plague the beginnings of all good things.

"And because only God could have sent Mary Eliza and Monsieur d'Yvetot when Sally needed them most," Mother said, "let us call the hill that overlooks our land Providence, for He has provided our help."

"And what about my cornhusk doll?" asked Sally. She was holding her precious poppet over little Jonathan, where he lay on the rag rug by the open door. "If I hadn't run away that day and chased the bears, and met Pretty Leaper, and gotten the doll, I might be in Canada this minute, being worked to death!"

"Don't let Jonathan pull it about," Mother warned. "*That* I want to be kept for your children's children. It's the wonder of the world!"

In a few days, word of Sally's return had spread as fast as horse and foot and voice could carry it. Adam told Si Gurney. That valiant neighbor, still at the cabin at the forks, told Secundus Dorp. Dorp had stubbornly rebuilt his cabin, burned the day of the raid, and even added a lean-to. He was a hardheaded German from Bird-in-Hand, back by Lancaster. Dorp carried wheat to the new mill, and there he met Aeneas MacDonald, the trader from South Branch. MacDonald was accompanied by the Reverend Obed Thrums, the Presbyterian preacher, who was making his yearly tour of the frontier. Of course, they heard about Sally, too.

So the news trickled up and down glades, over hogbacks, along runs. Wives and daughters put on their creased gowns that had been carefully stored in chests and presses. They brushed and braided the hair of wriggling, excited children. Men shaved bristling beards and resurrected cocked beaver hats and patched tail coats. Any event of such importance called for a "gathering."

Si Gurney, nursing a keg of cider on muleback, brought the word of it.

"God bless ye, Sally child," he shouted as the mule splashed across the run. "Kind of different from the last day I seed ye!"

He dismounted, beaming, and pumped Sally's hand.

"Why, you've growed! And fat and sassy as a partridge!

Blasted murderin' red devils!" he growled, pounding Henry Redpath's back warmly.

"But they brought her back, Master Gurney," Father said.

"They're not all devils," Sally defended her Indian family. "They were most kind. And they fetched me home safe."

"Hull passel o' folks're comin' to see ye, Sally," Si Gurney went on. "Good day to ye, Mistress Redpath. I hope ye got victuals for company."

Mother, with little Jonathan on her arm, smiled politely at Si Gurney. Sally knew from her absent-minded expression that she was worrying about food. No Callie to take care of the details of a feast; no Caesar to carry a market basket through the packed stalls of produce!

"Don't fret, Mother," Sally said. "We've got plenty. Adam's bringing a side of beef from Moyer's. He told me so this morning."

"I was but teasin', Mistress Redpath," said Si Gurney. "Everybody's fetchin' food along. Here, Master Redpath, put this cider in a cool spot. The last o' last year's squeezin's. A mite hard, but that'll be overlooked."

Matilda Redpath was flustered indeed, but not as much about the food as about the impression she might make on these simple folk who were coming perilous miles to do the family honor. Most of them were solid, sturdy people who had left barren farms or poverty-stricken homes in towns to seek their fortunes in the wilderness. Some of them were not so solid, either—there were always the shiftless, wandering ones who drifted gipsy-like across the frontier, looking for pots of gold beyond the next hill. In gingham and homespun and buckskin they would come, and share their little best with the Redpaths. And all the women would eye the hostess's gown. Would they think her too fine a lady? Would they envy the lace? Should she wear her blue shortgown with the embroidered lawn apron? And what should Sally wear?

The men were bothered with no such problems. Henry Redpath had fitted himself into the frontier picture better than anyone had dreamed he could. In his butternut-dyed shirt and kersey breeches, his unpowdered hair tied back with an eelskin, he looked little like Master Redpath, merchant, of Philadelphia.

Sally solved her own problem by announcing that she was going to wear her Indian dress. Luckily, it was a coolish day, and the deerskin skirt and loose top were not too warm.

After much mental struggle, Matilda Redpath donned her blue shortgown, a mobcap with real lace frills and a plain apron, and pinned her brooch with the crest at her throat.

Adam, Si Gurney and Father set up tables outside the cabin, by laying long planks on trestles. Adam hung the side of beef he had fetched from Moyer's in the shade, where it attracted almost as many flies as the meat-drying racks in the Shawnee village. He reported that the Moyers themselves, all six of them, were on their way, as well as the eleven Dorps and the McGinleys and Monahans.

The sun was slanting shadows for midafternoon when Sally spotted a line of people threading their way through the trees below the edge of Providence Hill.

"Them's Moyers," Adam said, squinting under his hand.

"Wonder he wouldn't give his woman a hand with them bundles she's totin'— By gorries, it's the twins!"

"Mistress Moyer is a strong woman," Matilda said, smiling ruefully. "She came six miles through the snow to help bring the baby for me, and a month later she had those twins."

"Did you go to help her?" asked Sally.

"She left word I was not to stir from this house until Jonathan was six weeks old. She thinks me a sickly city woman, I fear. I heard Mistress Dorp and Grandmother Jones from the mill were with her when her time came. 'Tis wonderful how folks help each other out here." Mother picked up Jonathan, straightened her cap, and went out to meet the neighbors.

CHAPTER

12

THE GATHERING

SALLY FELT SUDDENLY SHY, meeting all these strangers and being the reason for this "gathering." But the young Moyers surrounded her with solemn stares that soon melted into giggles. Mrs. Moyer, a broad, red-cheeked woman, cried out, *"Du lieber kind!"* and kissed her vigorously. Eli Moyer, a bearded German who reminded Sally of Jacob Stoltzfus without the beaming smile, grunted briefly at her, nodded at Father and Si Gurney, jerked his head stiffly at Mother, and sat down under a tree to smoke his pipe.

People came and came. Soon children were playing "I Spy" and "Here Come Three Lords Out of Spain" all over the place, men were clumped under trees, smoking and talking, and all the women were gathered near the cabin, oh-ing and ah-ing over Sally Redpath and the baby, comparing children's ailments, swapping recipes and the best way to dry apples or cure squirrel skins. Mother and a few of the women began to set out food. Just as Si Gurney had said, everyone had brought things to eat and drink, and soon the trestles groaned under platters of dried corn, fresh pone, home-cured bacon, honey, dried apple pies, venison steaks, fresh-caught fish, hominy and greens. Adam and the men had fires going behind the cabin to roast the beef. The cider keg was tapped. Someone drove in the cow and brought up a pail of warm, foaming milk for the children.

Dusk was beginning to fall, and Daffyd Jones, the Welsh miller, was tuning his fiddle for the dancing. But Si Gurney sprang up on the table and shouted for silence.

"Friends and neighbors," he called, "I reckon we all know why we're here today, an' that's to welcome back Miss Sally Redpath from her Injun captivity. I reckon lots of you has heard some of her story while you've been settin' with her and her ma. But so's not to tire her out with tellin' it over an' over, how about comin' up here, Miss Sally, an' tellin' it to us right now, if ye would be so kind?"

There were cries of "Oh, no, the poor little thing!" and "Hooray for Sally!" and "Si Gurney, air ye crazy?"

Mother whispered, "Sally, do you wish to?"

Sally felt very small and shy under the eyes of all that crowd. The men had come from under the trees and were standing with Father. The women were clustered around Mother and Grandmother Jones, who sat in her ruffled white Welsh bonnet with the tall black beaver hat that made her look like a good witch in a fairy tale. But the children—from the toddlers in their "togas" to the boys and girls in their patched frocks and worn leather breeches

—had stopped their noisy games and gathered in an eager clump at her feet.

Si Gurney, who seemed to have appointed himself master of ceremonies, hoisted Sally in her Shawnee dress onto the table. "Now, Miss Sally," he said, "I saw that Shawnee devil grab you right down there by the spring. He let out a tre-mendous whoop—"

Si Gurney got no farther. For over the run, out of the twilight, came an eerie screech that rivaled the Indian's and brought squeals from adults as well as children.

"The Lord help us, what's that?" cried Si, and then he laughed. The men lifted their heads, the women and children relaxed after that first involuntary shudder. Eager faces turned toward the run, as the wild music continued.

"The pipes, as I live and breathe!" exclaimed Father. "Surely the 42nd's not on the march?"

"That's MacDonald, the factor from South Branch," said Adam Byles. "He's got a set o' them heathen instruments. Aye, yonder he comes, an' he's got another man with him."

Out of the dusk emerged the figure of a marching man. How gallantly he came, the streamers on his pipes fluttering in the breeze, and waving behind him, from over his shoulder, a plaid of the MacDonald set. He was in full Highland dress, to the plumed bonnet and silver-mounted sporran. Thrust in his checkered hose was a handsome silver-hilted dirk. No man looked less like a storekeeper and trader and more like a Highland chief. Behind him, on a small brown mule, dressed in sober black-dyed homespun, rode a grave-faced man with straggling white hair.

The piper strode up to the group, tucked his instrument under his arm, doffed his bonnet and cried, *"Cead mhille*

failte, Mistress Redpath, which means 'a hundred thousand welcomes!'"

"Thank you, sir," Sally murmured, quite overcome by this gorgeous figure. He was as impressive as Seapessee in full war paint!

"And may I be presenting the Reverend Obed Thrums to ye all?"

The old man in black dismounted stiffly from his mule and made a bow to Matilda Redpath and Sally, a gesture of blessing and greeting to the assembly.

"This is a happy occasion, dear friends," he said, sitting down next to Grandmother Jones, who had risen and curtsied with great dignity. "And one on which I will later be moved to address ye. But I see we have arrived just in time to hear from this child who has been so mercifully restored to the bosom of her family. Speak, little one, speak!"

"Remind me to have business down by the spring when he gits launched on his sermon," muttered Adam to Secundus Dorp, who was standing by the chopping block with his three oldest boys.

So Sally began on her story once again. And when she wavered, eager listeners would always find a question that kept her going. They were a wonderful audience. Few of them could read or write, and here this little girl was telling a story that beat any romance in print, if they had been able to spell it out. They shuddered with her as she was dragged through the dark forest by Seapessee. They thrilled to the timely intervention of the cornhusk doll. Sally held it aloft, but it was getting dark, so, since even the men and boys wanted to see this "good medicine" that had saved her from a hard fate, she had to pass it around, with a plea to handle it carefully. One of the crawling Dorps almost pulled it in two, but it was rescued in time and handed back to Sally.

The neighbors listened with interest and surprise to her account of the winter with the Shawano. They made Adam tell again his oft-repeated end of the story of the letter and Lieutenant d'Yvetot. Mary Eliza McPhee had a flood of blessings called down on her head, and only a few of the women whispered in scornful undertones their opinion of "blanket women" who turned Injun. Sally didn't hear them, which was just as well for the whisperers. She was surprised to discover with what relief some of the men heard the part about Seapessee returning to dig up the bones of his ancestors.

"Yeah," said Johnston from Boiling Springs, a woodsman with years of Indian fighting to his credit (Adam had told Sally), "when they dig up them bones, they're pullin' out for good. Reckon we won't see no more of that band in these parts."

The people finally let Sally get down. After the last woman had inspected the dress that Macqua had made, and the last child had patted the cornhusk doll, she slipped inside the cabin with Mother. She took off the Shawnee dress and laid it carefully away. Then she put on her second-best dress of India mull. Somehow, she wanted badly to look very pretty and neat again. The other Sally, the Indian Sally, was being laid aside with the deerskin dress, never to be forgotten, but always to live a little apart.

When she went back out, it was full night. Daffyd Jones was tuning up in earnest now, and Aeneas MacDonald was making dronings on his pipes in the background. But before anyone could line up for the quadrille which was coming, the Reverend Obed was on his feet again, refreshed by a noggin of cider and a round of roast beef.

"Brothers and sisters," he began, spreading his hands for silence, "we are met, as I have said, on a most joyous occasion. The heathen have given up yet another lamb of the flock. Another Christian child has been restored to home and loved ones. I can see by the way some of my brothers in the back there are trickling off toward the woods that they fear I am about to preach a sermon. I will shame them by asking them if they think Providence would have looked upon their sinful souls in like benevolent manner, had they been the captives of the lost tribes of the forest? No, my people, the Lord shows us His manifold mercies in the saving of an innocent child. Oh, what a lesson is here, dear brethren!"

Oh dear, thought Sally. I really am very grateful to God for helping me get home, but am I being a wicked girl to wish the preacher didn't have to go on like that all evening? Then she remembered the Indian braves listening to the old man who told the story of Washa Manitou, in the lodge that winter night, and how politely all had listened to a story they had heard since childhood. I can do no less than be as polite as they, she told herself. So she sat meekly down on the ground with the young Dorps and Moyers, who were fidgety and given to whispering and poking each other.

Several pine knots had been lighted and stuck about, giving a red, flickering light to the scene. The gaunt figure of the minister, his arms upraised, rose over the group like an ancient prophet. Aeneas MacDonald, arms folded, leaned against the cabin door, shrouded in the tartan of the Lords of the Isles. The German settlers, used to their own pastor who preached the doctrine of Martin Luther in sonorous German, sat respectfully, although they understood little of the Reverend Thrums' exhortations. The Welsh Joneses, the Redpaths and several of the neighbors were Episcopalians. But all listened to the dominie, even Adam Byles, who always said if he went in a church, it would fall on him. His sneak down by the spring had been caught in time.

"Beware that he does not keep ye forever in his lodge in the forest of wrath! May good angels redeem ye, or else be sure ye were destined to the flames from the beginning." This was the kind of sermon his hearers were used to. They didn't want him to go on for hours, though. But, after all, Reverend Thrums only passed through once a year, and he seldom got this many people together in one spot. Grandmother Jones provided the opportunity for which they all were waiting. As the dominie paused for breath, she raised her wonderful Welsh voice, as strong as a young woman's, in the one tune she could have chosen that the whole group might sing. The words were Isaac Watts'—and all the Scots and English and Welsh would know them—but the tune was solid German—

> My feet shall never slide,
>   Nor fall in fatal snares,
> Since God, my guard and guide,
>   Defends me from my fears.
>
> Those wakeful eyes that never sleep,
> Shall Israel keep when dangers rise,
> Shall Israel keep when dangers rise.

The Dorps and Moyers caught the tune before they got to the second verse, as Grandmother Jones had hoped they would. Whatever words they sang made a sonorous undertone to the English lines. It caught them all up in a wave of strong feeling, better than any further preaching would have done. The Reverend Thrums, sensitive to the mood of his congregation, joined in lustily. At the end of the last verse, he simply said, "Amen! Amen!" and stepped down. It was a full minute before Daffyd's fiddle made a preliminary scrape....

The lines formed up right away for the quadrille. The cider was passed from hand to hand. The married folks and the children sat back and left the first figure to the pretty girls and young men—anybody over the age of twelve, it looked to Sally, and under forty. She was quite overcome, therefore, when a boy in his teens, all freckles and ears, in a clean flaxen shirt and blue breeches came over and said solemnly, "I'm John Fosdick. Will you dance with me, Miss Sally?"

Sally didn't know who this boy was, at all.

"Oh, thank you!" she gasped. "You're very kind."

And how the grown-ups smiled and whispered! Sally took the boy's hard brown hand. How glad she was now for the dancing lessons at Miss Collingwood's, though the stately quadrille in the long room in Philadelphia wasn't much like the lively affair that they swung into!

Daffyd Jones's fiddle glided gaily on, and now Aeneas MacDonald's skirling pipes put wings to their feet. Oh, what fun this was, Sally thought. How they bowed and turned and sashayed, up the line and down, while the onlookers nodded and tapped their feet! When it was over, and Sally had thanked John properly, he kept her hand for a moment as if she were a miss in her teens.

"I'm 'prenticed to Owen Jones, the miller's brother. I'm learning the coopering trade," he said. "Pa and Ma are dead. I'd be proud to have the next dance, too."

Sally looked at Matilda Redpath. Mother was smiling and nodding. And suddenly, Sally remembered another dance and another boy—a boy called The Raccoon, a dance in the snow before the Shawano lodges.

"I'd be pleased, Master Fosdick," she whispered. So this was what being grown up would be like! Across the next few years, Sally Redpath glimpsed the time when she would have outgrown the cornhusk doll—as a poppet to play with, of course, never as a treasure of very special memories.

"Come on, Welshman! Let's gie them a reel!" roared MacDonald, and the miller grinned from ear to ear. Swing your partners! Everybody round! Form a line and weave, like a snake round the clearing, with Johnston the woodsman leading the line, a flaming torch in his right hand and the oldest Dorp daughter clinging proudly to his left! "The Bringing Dance," thought Sally, racing along with John Fosdick ahead of her and a chubby Moyer behind. This was fun, this was life. Oh, how glad she was to be home!

Late, late that night, when most of the guests had straggled off in the wake of MacDonald, who was blaring "The Pibroch of Donal Dhu" in a manner calculated to scare any lurking Indians clear back to the Scioto, Sally lay in the trundle bed, worn-out and happy. Father and Mother were breathing gently in the four-poster. The Reverend Obed Thrums, after a fervent prayer, was bedded down on a comfortable pallet by the hearth. Little Jonathan lay in his cradle. Adam was snoring lustily in the loft. Outside, in the mild spring night, Johnston, John Fosdick and Owen Jones, who had stayed over, slept under the stars. The whippoorwills were clanging away on the hillside.

Sally breathed a sigh of deepest content. "I'll remember this day until I die," she told herself. But just before she drifted off to sleep, she felt beside her for the cornhusk doll. After all it would be many moons, as Pretty Leaper would have said, before she was too old to keep it by her day and night.

CHAPTER 13

THE MESSAGE

THE SUMMER CAME AND PASSED, with berrying and heat and thunderstorms. And then again there were the reddening leaves, the cornshocks and the chill mornings, the good feel of a linsey-woolsey gown, and Mother's knitted stockings.

On a frosty October evening, they were all seated around the fire. Father and Adam were mending traps and getting their winter gear in order, talking over the price of prime beaver and marten at a great rate. Mother was holding little Jonathan, who had come through his first summer in fine shape, a mercy in that time and place. Seven months old he was, and sitting up like a soldier. And crawl! He was too big for the cradle now. He could scramble over the side and onto the floor in a flash. So Sally had to share the trundle bed. She wasn't sorry. He would be a snug companion on cold nights. If only he didn't roll and toss so in his sleep! Sally had never dreamed a little baby could be so lively. As the fire crackled cheerfully and the men talked on, Sally's mind kept going back to this time last year. Seapessee and the braves were setting out on their bear hunt. She had just made friends with Mary Eliza McPhee. (A letter had gone to Uncle Jasper, by the way, carried by the Reverend Obed Thrums, and it was to be hoped that somehow the coveted India shawl could be transported to the Shawnee village by the hand of some westward-faring trapper or trader when it arrived in the spring.) And now, her own menfolk were getting ready for their autumn hunting, too.

Sally went and opened the cabin door. Over Providence Hill, hung a yellow harvest moon. It was so bright that she could see the water in Sore Trouble Run twinkling over the rocks. High, high overhead a familiar voice sent shivers down her spine. Leeakaw was on his way southward again. Yes, there across the face of the moon, sharply etched for a few seconds, was the V-shaped wedge of the wild goose flock. Tears smarted Sally's eyes. Something in the voice of the great birds, crying so strongly and triumphantly down the starlit sky, echoed in her own heart.

"Do you hear that, Father? Hear it, Mother, Adam? The geese are going South!"

"Aye," said Adam, rising and coming to stand in the doorway with her. "Means an early winter. Mighty glad we've got our roots set into this place, now. Seems like a man can draw a safe breath this year, without listenin' with one ear fer a war whoop."

Down in the woods, an owl hooted.

"Hear thet? Last year I'd 'a said thet was an Injun. This year, I'd lay even money on it's bein' an owl."

Sally laughed and went in to the fire.

It was in the dawn that she made the discovery. When she opened the door of the cabin, she saw something lying across it. Her cry of wonder brought the family on the run. There on the slab sill lay a fine, fat buck, fresh-killed. And in the wound—a magnificent heart-shot, too—was a Shawnee arrow!

Adam Byles stared wordlessly. Once again, the trapper was completely dumfounded.

"Right up to the door," he muttered. "Scalped in our sleep, we might have been."

"Oh, Henry!" Matilda Redpath whispered. "Do we have to go through that again?"

"Sillies!" cried Sally, "It was Seapessee! I know that arrow. I'm sure it's one I watched him make! Oh, don't you see? They passed by us in the night!"

"Aye," Adam admitted at last. "They'll make a gift that way."

"What's this?" Father asked, bending to pick up a small parcel wrapped in rawhide. They opened it cautiously, to find a round stone pendant, worn thin as a wafer with age, smooth as glass. On it were scratched crude pictures whose lines had been filled with earth, as though it had been long buried. The pictures showed suns with spreading rays, a tent-shaped mountain, stick-men and animals. The three examined it in wonder, trying to guess its meaning.

"It's not like what any of them wear," Sally said, puzzled.

"It's very old," Mother murmured, running her fingers over the smooth stone.

"It has been buried," Father guessed.

"Then it must be—it must mean that Seapessee found it

when he dug up the bones of his grandfather," Sally said slowly. "He wanted to try to tell us that he had found them? And he left the deer as a gift for us, too. That must be it. They've found the old fields. And now they're going home." Sally stood for a long while, gazing westward at the quiet woods. The Indians were going on—westward, ever westward, with the rising tide of the white strangers at their heels. The old fields that some day would be names on a white man's map—Shawnee Old Fields, Old Shawneetown—would be turned up by iron plowshare. The arrow points and broken pots that would puzzle children yet unborn—all these were being left behind again. It was saddening to think about, and a lump came in Sally's throat.

Then she lifted her hands toward the western woods. In one hand she held the cornhusk doll. In the other was the picture-stone. If they were watching now, as she felt they surely were—Seapessee, Macqua, Pretty Leaper, the Yelper —they could see her, they would know she was saying good-by for the last time.

"Come, Sally, mix the hoecake while I feed Jonathan," Mother called softly from within.

Sally Redpath put down the cornhusk doll and rolled up her sleeves. Her feet were set firmly, happily on another trail.

"I'm coming," she said.

The sun rose above Providence Hill in a blaze of glory.

ELEANOR REINDOLLAR WILCOX

winner of a *Dodd, Mead Librarian Prize Competition,* is a ninth generation Marylander and sixth generation Baltimorean. She studied art at the Maryland Institute of Art, library science at the Enoch Pratt Free Library and creative writing at Johns Hopkins University.

After four years as assistant to the library publicist and display expert in the Exhibits Department at the Enoch Pratt Free Library, she joined the staff of the Maryland Academy of Sciences as artist, lecturer, Curator of the Educational Film Library and Associate Curator of American Anthropology. Here her interest in Indian lore and customs led her to the books on colonial life in America and Trowbridge's classic account of life among the Shawnee which provided the authentic and fascinating background for her first book, THE CORNHUSK DOLL. This fine story of a little pioneer girl was a winner of the *Dodd, Mead Librarian Prize Competition.*

Following her marriage to a commercial artist, Eleanor Reindollar Wilcox joined her husband in business as Wilcox and Wilcox, Industrial Illustrators. Now Mrs. Wilcox is employed as Upper School Librarian at the Park School in Baltimore but she still finds time to serve as Cub Scout Den Mother for her two sons, George and David, help her husband build historical dioramas, paint portraits and landscapes, enjoy local history, wildlife and hiking and participate in amateur archeological projects.

"At present," Mrs. Wilcox says, "we are buying five acres in the country overlooking a beautiful lake formed by the new Liberty Dam, on the Patapsco River. It will take years to get the place in order, but we have put in an orchard of sorts and a vegetable patch, thinned timber, and maybe some day we will achieve a house!"

DEC 1957

DATE DUE			

HIGHSMITH 45 220

DEC 1957

Room 7